Not So Easy

THE *NOT* SERIES

TERRI OSBURN

Wall Street Journal Bestselling Author

Chapter One

STARING UP AT THE GREEN MONSTROSITY BEFORE ME, I couldn't help but smile. I finally did it. I bought a house. But not just any house. The one my grandparents, Rooster and Ethel Bradford—known to me as Pops and Bammy—built in 1975. The home that held all of my best memories, from weekends filled with baking, to summer evenings lounging on the porch swing. Sunday dinners, Christmas mornings, and endless Popsicles while Bammy braided my hair.

This had been my dream since the house was sold ten years ago. Then, I'd been fresh out of college with a fledgling photography business and no means to keep the house in the family. A decade later and it was finally mine. Unfortunately, it was also a catastrophe. Pops passed away well before Bammy and the home fell into disrepair in her later years, which was why no one in the family had been willing to take it over when she passed.

In the decade since, the place had changed hands three times, and no one bothered to put in the money, energy, or love needed to restore the simple two-story structure to its former glory. That changed now. I hadn't scrimped and saved all of these years for nothing. The cheap meals and extra jobs had been worth the sacrifice for this moment.

Now I needed the right person to help me transform the neglected mess into my dream home.

"You really did it," said a familiar voice from behind me.

Keeping my eyes straight ahead, my smile widened. "I told you I would."

Darnell stepped up beside me. He was my favorite cousin on my Dad's side, and held many of the same memories of this place as I did.

"Have you been inside?"

I bought the house as-is, sight unseen, but the pictures posted with the listing told me this was going to be a challenge. I didn't care. A little updating was all she needed.

"Not yet. I was waiting for you."

"Are you sure you're ready for this?" he asked.

Silly question. "More than ready."

We started up the short front walk, broken in places and nearly overtaken by weeds. The shrubs that served as a natural barrier enclosing the postage stamp-sized front yard would be the first things to go. They weren't original to the house, and they blocked much of the front porch.

"There's no power right now so we'll need the lights on our phones."

"Someone really liked green," Darnell muttered as we climbed the two steps onto the porch. "Is it green inside, too?"

"Thankfully, no." Running a finger along the dusty siding beside the door, I grimaced. "At least it's a light minty green. I plan to put it back to white, the way it used to be."

My cousin tapped the matching green metal awning shading the front of the porch. "Are you keeping these?"

Bammy had added those during my middle school years, and they were sorely outdated.

"No, those are going." I reached out to open the storm door and the knob came off in my hand. As Darnell squelched a laugh, I shrugged. "I plan to replace it anyway."

"Way to stay positive," he said, following me inside.

We both whipped out our phones and lit up the space, dust dancing through the beams of light as if angered by the disturbance. Making our way into the living room on the left, we explored in silence and I was grateful to Darnell for keeping his thoughts to himself. No doubt they were the same as mine, and I didn't need that kind of negativity spoken aloud.

To put it mildly, the place was a disaster. Every wall within sight had been painted a primary blue, and the trim bright white. Except whoever had done the job either hadn't used tape, or had applied it poorly, because the colors bled together in several places. There were cracks in the wall above the fireplace, one window was broken, and a ceiling fan dangled precariously from a single wire.

"I'll ask again," Darnell said in a hushed tone. "Are you sure you're ready for this?"

Too late to turn back now. "I knew it needed work."

He scoffed. "It needs gutted to the studs."

Leading the way into the kitchen, I barely managed to hold in a gasp. I did not remember it being *this* small. The counter on the back wall included the old stainless steel sink in the center, with roughly a foot of counter space on each side. How had we made all those breads and cookies with so little working area?

The window above the sink was intact, but filthy and covered by a mangled old blind. Most of the cabinet doors were gone, and the few that remained hung at odd angles.

Even if the doors were intact, the lower cabinets were bare wood and the uppers were white...laminate maybe? Someone had tried to improve this room and made all the wrong choices.

"The stove is in good shape," Darnell offered, digging deep for any way to be supportive. "Maybe you can open this up to the living room?"

That hadn't been in the original plan in my head, but it was now. "I'm hoping to increase the square footage by adding to the back of the house, but opening up this doorway is a good idea."

"You know what you need?" my cousin asked. A match was the first thing that came to mind. "Calvin Hopkins," he added as I swallowed my negative thought. "He knows this neighborhood as well as we do, and he's been flipping houses on this street for the last couple of years."

My cousin was forgetting one important factor. "Calvin Hopkins hates me."

Darnell frowned. "No, he doesn't."

"Um...yes, he does. He's always hated me."

I wished I could say the same, but there had been those years during middle and high school when I must have written Donna Hopkins in my Girl Power notebook a couple thousand times. The combination of Calvin growing into those broad shoulders and my runaway hormones had short-circuited my brain. I was young and dumb, and could not be held accountable for my temporary bout of teenage puppy love induced insanity.

"That's not how I remember it." He arched one dark brow while smiling like a fool.

"What is that look about?"

After sliding a finger across the dirty Formica, he brushed the dust off on his jeans. "You two were like a match and gasoline. He'd tease you, and you'd go off like a Roman candle." Shaking his head, he added, "It was always so obvious. I'm still amazed y'all didn't end up together."

"You need to check your memories again. That isn't how things were *at all.*"

Calvin and I had created sparks all right, but not the type Darnell insinuated. If I said the sky was blue, Calvin would have argued that it was green just to tick me off. When I suggested we all get pizza, he'd push for burgers. Stroll down to Sylvester's on the corner for ice cream? Nope. Calvin would insist we head for the convenience store for pop and peanuts. An extra four blocks away, I might add.

"You know what?" Darnell said, turning his phone around and shining the light directly into my eyes. "I bet he's around."

Holding up a hand to save my eyesight, I stepped back and bumped into the dilapidated cabinets. A door hit the floor beside my foot, sounding like a gun shot and taking several years off my life.

"What are you doing?" I asked once my heart rate lowered.

"Yo, Calvin, it's Darnell. Donna and I are up here at Bammy's place." After a brief pause, he laughed. "Yeah, she bought it. Now she needs someone to save it. Can you come take a look?"

Cursing under my breath, I tried to reach for his phone, growl whispering, "What the hell, Dar?"

He fended me off and kept talking. "Cool cool. We'll meet you on the porch." He ended the call and gave me a smirk that made me want to clean the counter top with his face. "He's on his way."

"I have no intention of hiring Calvin Hopkins to renovate this place. Changing out a few appliances and adding new flooring doesn't make him a contractor qualified to do what I want to accomplish here."

"You obviously haven't seen his website. Remember Hickamore House? The one that was barely standing down on the corner? Who do you think saved it?"

Annoyed, I marched back into the living room. "He probably hired a real contractor."

"Cal *is* a real contractor," Darnell said, following behind me. "He's good, and he cares about this neighborhood. Plus, you *know* him. Why hire some dude off the internet when you've got an old friend right here on the street that you already know you can trust?"

Old friend was a stretch. More like old enemy. Well, enemy might be too strong a word, but barely tolerable acquaintance for sure.

I'd passed Hickamore House on my way here and had to

admit I'd been amazed at how good it looked. The sign out front declared it a wedding venue. Very smart way to make the renovation money back, since no one was likely to live in a house that large.

Doubtful Calvin did the renovation on his own. There must have been a pro in charge. I could use a good recommendation, so I begrudgingly agreed to the impromptu meeting.

"Fine, I'll hear what he has to say."

Not quite under his breath, Darnell mumbled, "You always were the stubborn one."

"I heard that."

Spinning to walk backward in front of me, he smirked again. "Am I wrong?"

Unwilling to incriminate myself, I embraced my right to remain silent.

As we waited for Calvin, I surveyed the rotted boards that made up most of the front porch and tried to remember how long it had been since I'd seen my childhood nemesis. If memory served, we'd crossed paths at a Pirates game recently. Four years ago, or maybe five. So not *too* recent. We hadn't talked then. He'd been in line at a concession stand and hadn't noticed me as I passed by. I didn't bother saying hello. I can't deny that he looked good, but then Calvin always had.

Not liking him didn't mean I was blind.

"Hey, man," Darnell said, snapping me back to the present. "Thanks for coming over."

"You caught me at a good time," Calvin replied, voice low and smooth and far too intoxicating for my liking. Had he always sounded that way? Like a fine brandy on a cold winter's night?

I gave myself a mental head slap. One sentence and he had me waxing poetic.

Get. A. Grip.

"You remember Donna, right?" my cousin said, shooting me that dang smirk again. I didn't know if he was testing me, Calvin, or both of us.

Calvin nodded. "Sure I do. Been a long time, though. You don't come around the neighborhood much anymore." Glancing around, he added, "That's why I was surprised to hear you bought the place."

The words carried a hint of judgment. An accusation that maybe I thought this area was beneath me. I didn't like to be judged, and I found the accusation insulting.

"I always wanted to keep this house in the family. That's what Bammy would have wanted, too. It just took me a while to make it happen." I crossed my arms. "I've never forgotten where I came from."

With a smile that sent me reeling, he gave another nod. "Good." Again surveying his surroundings, Calvin whistled. "You've got your hands full with this one."

"It's bad," Darnell confirmed. "Wait 'til you see the inside."

"I have."

"What?" How could that be? "When were you inside?"

He shrugged. "I did a walk-through before I put in my offer."

"Your offer?" I repeated.

He leaned against a porch post. "My mission is to restore the neighborhood. When a house on the block goes up for sale, I go after it." His casual stance paired with the nonchalant statement made my jaw tighten.

I knew I'd been up against another buyer, but I'd had no idea that buyer was Calvin.

"You tried to buy this place?" Darnell asked with a chuckle. "I should have known. It's no surprise you backed out. This house will take a miracle to save."

Calvin shook his head and straightened. "The work involved wasn't the issue. So why'd you call me over?"

"He shouldn't have bothered you," I cut in before Darnell could respond. "I've got things handled here."

Darnell was undeterred.

"Will you stop being so stubborn?" Turning to Calvin, he said, "I told her you're the perfect person to fix this place up. You know the neighborhood, you do great work, *and* you're like part of the family." I huffed at that, but Darnell ignored me. "Nobody else is going to care about this house as much as we do."

"We?" I cut in. "Your name isn't on the mortgage."

Growing serious for once, he shot me the Bradford look. The one that said I'd crossed a line. To be fair, I had. This was the family home, no matter whose name was on the deed.

"Sorry." Pointing out the obvious, I said, "I'm sure Calvin has a full schedule of his own projects. I can find someone else to do the work."

Knowing he'd nearly taken the home out from under me set my teeth on edge. What if he'd kept bidding? What if he'd won? I didn't want to think about it, and I didn't want to work with him. Just standing here was making me all too aware of how attractive he was.

"I've got the time," he said, dark brown eyes locked on mine.

With a slight panic, I searched for any excuse to end this. As much as I didn't want to hire him, I also had no desire to insult him.

"I'll need to collect multiple quotes. If you want to submit one, you're welcome to do so."

And then I would gleefully pick someone else. Someone who didn't make me want to throttle them but also bake them cookies at the same time. Baking was my love language. Other than photography, it was the one thing I was good at thanks to Bammy's lessons, all of which took place in this house.

Gesturing toward the front door, Calvin said, "I'll need to know what you envision for the project. Can we do a walk-through?"

Part of me wanted to say no. I loved this house so much that I hated for anyone to see it in the current condition. But then I remembered he'd already been inside. If he'd still put in an offer after that, maybe the place wasn't as bad as I feared.

"We can do that."

Instead of leading the way with an *I told you so* swagger, Darnell stepped around Calvin and descended the porch steps. "I've got to head out."

"Where are you going?" I called as he sped down the sidewalk. If this was nothing more than a ruse to get Calvin and me alone together, I was going to make sure Darnell paid.

"I promised Tiff I'd be back to mow the yard."

Tiff was Darnell's wife. They'd been together since high school. He'd spent all of freshman year trying to catch her attention, but it wasn't until the middle of sophomore year that she finally noticed. They'd been together ever since.

My watch read barely past noon. He had plenty of time for the yard, but before I could point this out, he'd already closed the chain link gate and was sauntering down the block.

Turning to Calvin, I said, "That fence and these shrubs are the first to go."

"Noted." He pulled a small notebook and a pen from the chest pocket of his well-worn overalls.

"Do you always have a notebook with you?" Had he and Darnell conspired on this little meeting? Why else would he come prepared to take notes?

"You never know when you'll need to write something down."

I couldn't argue with that. "All right, then. Follow me."

Chapter Two

Stopping in the small foyer, I whipped out my phone and switched on the light. Like some handyman magician, Calvin pulled a flashlight out of who knew where and lit up the entire space.

Again, he seemed a little too prepared for this impromptu meeting.

"So you have a notebook *and* a flashlight?"

"You never walk through a flip without a flashlight," he said.

"But you didn't know you were going to walk through a flip." This was feeling more and more like a setup by the second.

As if he could read my mind, Calvin shook his head. "I don't remember you being so suspicious. I get calls about houses all the time. Being prepared is part of the job."

A likely excuse, but I let it slide. For now.

"The stairway will need to be fully restored, obviously," I

said, shining my meager phone light at the partially paint covered banister. Who would paint over that gorgeous wood?

"You want it back to the original stain?"

"Yes." Leading the way into the living room, I pointed my light at the floors. "New floors throughout. Hardwood or I'm okay with a luxury vinyl, both upstairs and downstairs. No carpets."

"Not even in the bedrooms?" he asked.

"Nope." I braced for an argue, but he kept his thoughts to himself. "New paint, of course. And what about those?" I asked, shining my light on the cracks above the fireplace.

"Not sure. I'd have to get up there and take a closer look. Didn't the fireplace used to be brick from floor to ceiling?"

"That's how it was when I was a kid, yeah. And the mantel had been a full surround. Not just a beam like it is now."

I had adored Bammy's fireplace. We never had one in our apartment, which left nowhere to hang the stockings. Bammy made sure every grandchild had one here, each adorned with our names. Where they were now I had no idea, but the memory tightened my chest.

Fixing up this house wouldn't bring Bammy back, but it *would* restore her legacy, and regain a piece of the past that we never should have lost.

"You want it back the way it was?"

"I'm still debating." Concerned, I asked, "If I do, is that possible?"

Calvin flashed his perfectly straight pearly-whites. "Anything is possible."

My chest tightened again, but not from nostalgia. Clearing my throat, I continued the tour.

When we reached the next room, I sighed. "I don't remember the kitchen being this small. I need to extend the house out into the the backyard or there's no way to have a functional kitchen."

"Plenty of rentals have kitchenettes. We could make that work in here."

I bristled. "This isn't going to be a rental. I plan to live here, and I'm going to need a real kitchen."

Dark eyes widened. "You're going to *live* here?"

Why did he think I bought the place? Bammy's house wasn't meant to be a source of income. It was meant to be a home. *My* home.

"Yes. You have a problem with that?" Too bad if he did.

"Like I said, you don't come around much."

Annoyed, I decided to clear this issue up once and for all. "If you recall, I never lived here. I came to visit Bammy, and once she was gone, I didn't have much reason to be here."

"You have three cousins living within a couple blocks of here, and you had friends. Or at least we thought you did."

We? Did he think *we* were friends? My phone wasn't blowing up with invitations over the last ten years. Not from him or anyone else.

"Not that I need to defend myself, but I've attended multiple wedding showers, baby showers, birthday parties, and cookouts at my cousins' homes. If anyone else wanted to invite me to an event, they would have had no problem finding me."

Calvin matched my tone. "So you need an invitation to hit the neighborhood? There has to be an event?"

What the hell? "Yes, Calvin. We're grown-ups now. I'm not going to stroll the street knocking on doors asking if my friends can come out to play."

"You always saw yourself as better than the rest of us."

That one came out of nowhere. "What are you talking about? When I was here, I was as much a part of the neighborhood group as you were. Not that you didn't do your best to keep me out."

Calvin dropped his arms, casting the space into darkness. "I never tried to keep you out."

"Then you and I have very different versions of the past." Marching back to the foyer, I mumbled, "This is a waste of time."

"Do you know why I stopped bidding on this house?" he asked, following close behind me.

"I assume because the work required is above your skill level." Slamming through the creaky screen door, I stepped onto the porch.

Sadly, he caught the door before it hit him in the face. "I quit because I found out *you* were the other bidder." He paused as if to let that news sink in. "I work hard to make sure these houses don't go to developers who only see them as a means to an end. People who don't care if the work is done right. All they want is to get tenants in and start making money."

"From what you said inside, you think that's what I planned to do."

Calvin ran a hand over his cropped hair. "Yes, I thought

you were going to rent it out, but I knew you'd make sure the renovations were done right, and that you'd rent to quality people. No shoddy work and then becoming an absentee landlord, doing nothing to maintain the place."

In his world, I assumed this was a compliment.

"But I would never live in it myself. Seeing as I think I'm better than the other people in this neighborhood."

Without hesitation or remorse, he nodded. "That was the assumption, yeah."

Did others on the block feel the same? Was that why I never heard from anyone other than family? I'd worked day and night after college to build my business. Any job that came my way, I took. There hadn't been time for a social life. So no, I hadn't sought out old friends in those days. That didn't mean I looked down on them. I was busy.

"You assumed wrong, and there's no need to waste any more of our time. The one thing you got correct is that I *will* make sure the work is done right. By someone *other* than you."

Opening his mouth as if to argue, Calvin paused, and then closed it. "I'm here if you have any questions."

"I won't."

A lie, most likely, but there were plenty of other sources I could turn to in this process. Like the whole freaking internet.

Lips pursed, Calvin glanced around the porch. "I look forward to seeing it when it's done." I almost replied *fat chance* but bit the words back. On his way off the porch, he said, "Adding on in the back is a good idea. It'll be a lot of work, but don't let anyone tell you it can't be done."

First he insulted me and now he wanted to be helpful? Pick a lane.

When I didn't respond, he took the hint and marched his denim-clad butt off my property. He'd see. Once I found a contractor, the result would be better than anything Calvin Hopkins could have come up with. All I had to do was find the *right* person for the job.

———

"I'M NEVER GOING to find a contractor for this job," I lamented to my four best friends as we gathered for Sunday morning breakfast at our favorite Mexican restaurant. We were a bit addicted to their Huevos Rancheros.

"You'll find the right one," Becca assured me. "Just be patient."

At eight months pregnant, Becca Kim could barely get close enough to the table to reach her water glass. She'd taken forever to develop the slightest baby bump, but once the little one had really started to grow Becca had been waddling in no time.

"I agree," said Megan. "Someone will come along soon."

Becca and Megan Knox had much in common. Both were tiny. Both were madly in love. And both were endearingly optimistic. While the other three members of our group —Josie Danvers, Lindsey Pavolski, and myself—were more rooted in reality. Falling in love had added a tad more sunshine to Josie's world view, but she could still be counted on for the occasional bout of cynicism.

"I've contacted six contractors so far. Two never called

me back, and two turned down the job outright, claiming their schedules are booked for the rest of the year." Which seemed odd considering it was only April. "Another gave me an estimate well above what I paid for the house, and the last one wanted to tear the whole thing down and start over."

"All men, I assume," Lindsey said. "You need to hire a woman."

I loaded a bite of egg onto my fork. "I tried. She's one of the ones with a full schedule."

"Miles says he doesn't know anyone," Josie offered. "When I suggested we lend out Evan he got all grumpy. He can build anything, but Miles needs him at the company."

The company was a children's party planning business that Miles Porter built out of nothing to become the premier source for kid celebrations in Pittsburgh. Thankfully, Becca's employer—also an events company—didn't handle kid events so the two weren't direct competitors. Miles had been Josie's first client when she started her bookkeeping business last year.

I admired anyone who built a thriving business out of nothing, having done the same myself. Connecting with Becca had been a turning point in Bradford Photography. She'd been a work associate first, directing the majority of her wedding-planning clients my way, before we progressed into a ride or die friendship.

A few months later she introduced me to the other ladies at the table. Josie and Megan were Becca's college friends, while she and Lindsey had been close since grade school. The rest was history.

"What about you, Lindsey? Could you ask your dad? After forty years as a plumber, surely he knows someone."

Linds was a high school English teacher and the most down to earth person I knew. She was a realist, a bit of a pessimist, and unwaveringly loyal to her friends. Stuffing a bite of fried tortilla into her mouth, she took the time to chew before answering.

"I did," she said once the food was down. "He says all his old cronies are retired like he is. Between playing pickleball and watching every televised sporting event known to man, he hasn't kept up with the new guys in the industry."

Reality set in. I was going to be left with only one option. The one I'd rather die than go crawling back to, especially after our last encounter. In hindsight, I had to admit I hadn't been the best version of myself that day.

Maybe it was the rejection from fifteen years ago. Not that I'd ever told him how I felt, but I *had* made myself available. I showed up in places when I knew he'd be there. Made sure he knew when I got my first cell phone, hoping he'd ask for my number. When the spring formal came around, I turned down three different guys, sure that Calvin would ask me instead.

He never did.

The notebook doodling had stopped after that, and I made the most of the rest of my high school years with casual boyfriends, parties, and the typical harmless trouble that teenagers stumbled into. Maybe it was true what they said about first loves. Even when it's only puppy love, we never forget how they made us feel.

Tossing a piece of chorizo into my mouth, I embraced the

positive statements from earlier. "The right one is out there. Tomorrow I'll start calling around again."

Calling everyone *but* Calvin Hopkins.

"Will the house have a space for your business?" Becca asked.

Currently, I rented a large loft that was big enough for both my home and my office. With the high ceilings and loads of natural light, it was the perfect space for a photography studio. Retaining the apartment for the business alone wasn't financially feasible.

"It will, yeah. I'm putting on an addition that will give me a new kitchen with a studio above it. Parking might be an issue, but hopefully clients won't mind that so much."

My current building offered a parking lot, which made it convenient for visiting clients, but Bammy's house came with street parking only. There was a small parking area in the back, but that would be greatly reduced with the addition to the house.

Lindsey voiced the reality I'd been trying to ignore. "This is going to be a big change."

The negatives hung in the air. Less space. Less convenience. Both of which meant potentially less income. Was I putting nostalgia over common sense? Insisting on making this house work at the expense of what I'd spent a decade building?

"Change isn't a bad thing," I said, almost believing my own words. "This is nothing more than a relocation, and the new studio will be even better than the one I have now." Not a lie if I was able to put in the window package I wanted.

"The house is less than two miles from my apartment so no one can complain about having to drive too far."

My friends exchanged glances and I knew what they weren't saying. The move might be only two miles, but into a less desirable neighborhood. My loft was in the heart of an already rejuvenated part of Southside. Though the building was nearly a century old, great care had been taken to make it look as contemporary as possible while maintaining much of the original charm.

And when I was done with Bammy's house, it would be just as inviting. I could put a business entrance in the back, and hopefully retain a parking space next to the detached garage. The alley behind the house wasn't too narrow. And the house wasn't hard to find with GPS.

So the move wasn't ideal. I could make it work. I had to. This house was as much my dream as my business had been a decade ago. If having both required a little compromise, then so be it.

Chapter Three

"Once you find a contractor, do you know what all you want to do with it?" Megan asked. "When Dad redid his kitchen, I couldn't believe how many decisions he had to make." Reaching for her Bellini, she added, "There must be a thousand options for cabinet hardware alone. How does anyone choose?"

I *was* overwhelmed when the initial planning started, but using the house's original features as a reference helped cut down the options. There was still a million and one decisions to make, but focusing on one room at a time minimized the overload.

"I'm creating a storyboard that includes colors, textures, and the overall feel for each space, but I'm waiting until I lock down a contractor to work on the kitchen and bathrooms, since those will require way more choices."

Right now the main bath on the second floor was the only one in the house. The primary bedroom would get an ensuite, and there needed to be a powder room added downstairs.

Clients who visited the studio would use the existing bath, which meant it needed to be really nice when we were done.

"What about you?" I said to Megan. "How's the wedding stuff coming?"

At Becca's reception in January we learned that Megan's boyfriend—now fiancé—had given her a ring earlier that week. Since she wanted a fall wedding this year, the planning had moved into high gear.

"Becca is doing most of the work," she said. "Though Miriam is constantly bringing me pictures and ideas." Miriam was Megan's boss and I would never not love that the director of a library was named Miriam Webster. "Another plus of working in a library," she said. "Lots of resources."

"So far we have colors and the date," Becca said. "Venues are still being explored, but we need to lock one in soon. Six months out a lot of places are already booked."

"Are you aiming for Southside?" Lindsey asked.

That's where Megan's dad lived and where she and Ryan had an apartment together. Though I could name dozens of venues all over town, I typically left the recommending to Becca. She dealt with the staff of these places and knew where to go and where *not* to go.

Megan popped a piece of egg into her mouth. "I'd like that, but I'm also open to other areas. The church where Becca got married is beautiful, but it's booked the rest of the year. Another one I like is a bit of a drive, but we're going to see it this afternoon. It's out in Darlington."

"Where is that?" Josie asked.

"Above Beaver Falls," Becca replied. "Which reminds

me, we're taking Sophie to the zoo next weekend, if anyone else wants to come. Jill and her guy will be there, too."

Sophie was Becca's seven-year-old step-daughter. Against all odds, Becca and Jill, Sophie's mother and Becca's husband's first wife, had become good friends. The two couples even went on the occasional double date.

I wasn't sure I could do the same in Becca's situation, but I'd also met Jill and really liked her.

Lindsey scoffed. "How did that remind you of the zoo?"

"Beaver," Becca said, as if this made perfect sense.

"Do they have beavers at the zoo?"

"They do." She stacked salsa onto a chip. "We had a wedding there two weeks ago, so Marquette and I took the opportunity to walk around."

"There you go," Josie said. "Have your wedding at the zoo."

Megan shook her head. "It's booked for the next *two* years."

"That sucks." I rarely entered the picture before such details were locked down so I wasn't much help. "I'm sure the perfect place will open up. Becca would likely know before me, but if I hear of a sudden cancellation, I'll pass it along."

"I appreciate that. Both Becca and Ryan keep telling me it'll work out so I'm not going to stress about it." The eye twitch said otherwise, but there was no need to be discouraging.

"What if you don't find one before Becca pops?" Lindsey asked. The poor woman already looked ready to burst. "There's only two weeks left before the little tyke makes his appearance."

The expectant mother leaned back and patted her protruding belly. "I'm sure we'll find one by then, but if not, Amanda will take over. She's already handling most of my summer clients." Her shoulders rose and fell with a sigh. "I can't even take a deep breath anymore. The doctor says if he keeps growing at the current rate, we might induce a week early."

We all sat up straighter.

"Really?" Josie said. "We could be holding him as soon as next week?"

She laughed. "You'll have to get in line behind Jacob, Sophie, and Mom and Dad, but yeah. Next week." Her eyes locked on her water glass. "Wait. I could be a mom *next week*."

The rest of us exchanged glances, surprised by the sudden panic. She'd had nearly nine months to process the situation. Not as if this was new news.

"That's a good thing, right?" Lindsey said, using a voice usually reserved for disgruntled toddlers. "No more heartburn, constant peeing, and kicks in the kidneys."

Becca's eyes were wide as she looked up. "But then he'll be...out here." Tiny hands gestured wildly in the air. "I'm not ready for that."

"Sure you are, sweetie." Josie rubbed her back. "You've done the classes and decked out the nursery and bought the cute clothes. All that's left is to meet the little guy."

"But then I have to take care of him. Feedings and burpings and diaper changes. What if I drop him? What if he doesn't like me?"

A bit irrational, but I remembered when Darnell's wife was expecting their first. She'd been similarly freaked out.

"Becca, he's going to have the best mom in the world. You aren't going to drop him, and of course, he'll love you." Motioning to the others at the table, I added, "Plus, you have us. And Jacob *and* your parents. A whole baby posse ready and willing to help out."

This appeared to reassure her. "That's true." She relaxed into her chair. "It's just...a lot."

"It is," Megan agreed. "But you've got this. Imagine him smiling up at you for the first time. Or wrapping his itty bitty fingers around your thumb. Oh, and that new baby smell when you sniff the top of his head." Voice wistful, her brown eyes glazed over.

"You want one, too, don't you?" Josie teased.

The daydreaming librarian snapped back to the present. "Well, I mean...someday, yeah."

"There isn't anything you aren't telling us, is there?" Lindsey said.

The rest of us watched Megan intently.

Ponytail swinging as she shook her head, she said, "You know if I was pregnant I'd never be able to keep it a secret. Look how bad I was at hiding the ring?"

Good point. The goal had been to let Becca have her day and tell us about the engagement after, but Megan didn't make it through the reception.

"Don't rush into it," Becca said, slowly lifting off her chair. "I've peed more in the last week than in the last decade, and I'm pretty sure my internal organs are squeezed into the only two inches of space this baby isn't taking up."

The fact that any woman did this more than once was an absolute miracle.

"He'll be here soon, hon," Josie said. "Then all your organs can go back into place."

Becca grumbled as she waddled off toward the bathroom.

"That poor woman," Lindsey said, pulling her debit card from her back pocket. "Little Noah needs to cut his mom a break and get out here."

"For real," Josie said. "Watching her go through this helps reinforce my decision not to have kids."

"You don't think you'll change your mind?" Megan asked.

"No, ma'am."

"What about you, Donna?" she asked me. "Where do you stand on having kids?"

As an only child, I'd bounced around on this issue over the years. There were moments of loneliness in my childhood that made me think that if I did become a mother, I'd be sure to have more than one. Then there were times I watched the news and couldn't imagine bringing another human into this mess of a world.

There was also the fact that I was eternally single with no prospects on the horizon.

"For now, I'll work on birthing this house and deal with anything beyond that if or when the time comes."

"At least the house won't rearrange your organs," Lindsey pointed out.

That was a plus. "I have a feeling there will still be labor pains involved."

"Oh," Megan said, pushing in her chair. "Maybe you'll

find a hot contractor that will make you want to have *his* babies."

The others laughed while Calvin's sexy smile, dark eyes, and broad shoulders danced through my mind. I had to admit, the man would make beautiful babies. Shaking the thought away, I tossed a tip onto the table.

"All I want out of this project is a finished house. Once I have that, hot or otherwise, the contractor can go on his merry way."

Josie tucked her arm around mine as we walked toward the exit. "Would it be so bad to keep your options open?"

I thought of Calvin again. "Yes. Yes, it would."

———

Days passed with the group chat on baby alert. Becca grew more miserable, while also doing her best not to whine. If anyone deserved a little whine—and wine, actually—it was her. Because of the uncertainty of baby Noah's arrival, the zoo trip had been postponed. The venue visit they'd done after breakfast had also been a bust, so the wedding venue hunt continued.

"I've had a look around," said Walter, the latest contractor assessing the house. "It'll be a miracle if you get the permits needed, and the work required to secure the foundation to take on the extra weight will likely blow your budget. Your best bet is to rework what you've got standing and try to get your money back by selling this heap off to someone else."

Walter was clearly *not* the man for the job.

"Thank you for your time," I said before spinning on my heels and opening the gate. "You have a good day."

Understanding the unspoken response, he said, "You won't find anyone willing to do what you want."

I closed the gate behind him. "We'll see." There was no point in arguing, though I was beginning to fear he might be right. Staring up at the house, I sighed. "There has to be someone willing to take you on."

"Still no luck?" said a voice behind me, scaring me half to death.

Spinning, I found Calvin with his hands tucked into his overalls and a knowing grin on his face. "Do you always sneak up on people like that?"

He ignored my question. "Walt was a no, huh?"

Crossing my arms, I tried not to grind my teeth. "He says I should repair what's here and sell the *heap* to someone else."

"Ouch. That's harsh."

Yes, it was. "Doesn't matter. I'll find the right contractor."

Rocking from toes to heels, he said, "I'm still available."

I bit back the response dancing at the tip of my tongue. Walter had been the only one to return my call in the last week. My options were quickly dwindling, and I'd already considered hiring Calvin. There was my pride and then there was the house. I could sacrifice the one to save the other. At least he'd saved me the embarrassment of having to call and beg him to come back.

Curious, I said, "Why do you want this job so badly?"

"I told you before. I care about this street. I also think you've got some good ideas about what the place needs."

Pulling a folded up paper from his back pocket, he said, "I drew up a quote, just in case you changed your mind."

I accepted the paper and read it over. It included everything we'd discussed the day we walked around, plus a couple of things I knew I hadn't mentioned but that were definitely on my list. This smelled of Darnell again, since he and I had discussed the plans just two days ago.

The weight of reality settled in. Calvin really was my only option.

"You can get the permits?" I asked. "Including for the addition?"

He nodded. "Yes, ma'am."

"What about the foundation? Walt said we'd need to do extra work so it'll support the new part."

Eyes narrowed, he pondered the question. "That depends. Do you want to extend the basement under the addition, or stick with what you have and make the new section a crawl space?"

I'd only thought about the stuff above ground, not below it. "What would you do?"

Rubbing his chin, he stared at the house behind me. "Personally, I'd keep it how it is and stick with building from the ground up."

That felt right to me. I couldn't believe I was about to say this.

"Fine, you have the job."

Instead of the smug look I expected, he offered a genuine smile. "Are you sure?"

Did I have a choice? "Yes, I'm sure."

Calvin extended his hand. "Then I accept."

The moment our hands touched my whole body went warm as if I was back in high school about to melt at the feet of my teenage crush.

"Good," I said, clearing my throat and pulling my hand away. "I'd like to get started as soon as possible."

I had enough money to pay both the mortgage and the rent for four months, and I'd already lost two weeks trying to find a contractor.

"Do you have time to meet tomorrow?" he asked.

Whipping out my phone, I checked my calendar. "I have clients in the studio at ten and two, but I can meet in between."

"Great," he said. "I'll send you the address."

"We aren't meeting here?"

He shook his head. "We can't do anything without blueprints. Meet me at the address I send you at eleven thirty."

"Okay," I said as he walked away. Watching him go, I muttered, "Four months tops. Then he'll be back out of your life."

Four. Long. Months.

Chapter Four

THE SIGN ON THE BRICK BUILDING READ *STEEL CITY Print & Design*. Once I stepped inside, it took several seconds for my eyes to adjust from the bright sun outside to the dim interior. Still a bit blinded, I heard a voice call my name but struggled to see who it was.

Then the person drew closer and my vision cleared. "Sheilah Watts? Is that you?"

Sheilah grew up on Bammy's street, but I hadn't seen her since maybe a year after high school. Last I heard she'd gone to design school, but I'd assumed that meant fashion design.

"It is," she said, tossing long braids over her shoulder. "Donna Bradford? What brings you in here?"

"I do," said Calvin, entering the showroom. "You're on time," he said with a wink. "I appreciate that." Why would I not be on time? "Sheilah, those plans I sent you yesterday are for Donna's grandmother's old place. We're flipping it."

The "we" part hit me wrong. *I* was flipping the house. *He* was the hired hand.

"Really?" Sheilah said. "Good for you. That'll make a great income property."

This again.

"It won't be an income property," I explained. "I'm going to live there."

Confusion in her eyes, she looked from me to Calvin and back. "You're going to live *in* the neighborhood?"

"Yes."

Not one to explain myself, I left it at that. She again looked to Calvin as if he would explain the mystery. There was no mystery, but he clearly wasn't the only person who'd made incorrect assumptions about me.

After an awkward silence, Calvin said, "Can we look at the prints?"

"Oh, yeah." She snapped into motion. "They're laid out over here."

We followed her to a large table off to the left. She unrolled the blueprints, then used paper weights to hold down each corner. "It's rare to get originals like this. At least for homes in our area."

I'd sent a request to the city for the original plans and gotten nowhere. "How did you get these?"

He leaned over the large paper. "I have plans for nearly every house within our four block area. You never know when one will go up for sale and I like to be ready."

Well, wasn't he Mr. Prepared.

Leaning next to him, I noticed how good he smelled. Like what I imagined the ocean must smell like. Salty and fresh and soothing. Stopping myself from taking a deeper breath, I asked, "Does this have the full lot?"

"It does." Making a box with his finger, he said, "This is where we'll put the addition. If you don't care about having a garage, we can take the detached one out to still leave you some yard."

No longer having to scrape snow off my car took priority over a yard. "I'd rather keep the garage, but we can take it down from a two-car space to a one-car." Pointing to the half of the garage next to the single parking spot, I said, "I only want enough space to have a nice fire pit area here."

He nodded. "That's doable." To Sheilah he said, "Do you have the reworked ones ready?"

Reworked ones? Wasn't reworking them the point of this meeting?

"Sure." She unrolled more documents and placed them on top of the originals, using the same weights to hold the corners. "First floor is on top and the second floor is on the bottom."

There on the table was Bammy's house, only better. Almost a direct reflection of the version I saw in my head. The larger kitchen with the wall gone between it and the living room. The powder room squeezed in below the stairs, and even a deck added behind the addition.

Part of me was amazed that he'd gotten so many details right, while another was annoyed that he'd taken it upon himself to make the changes. Looking closer, I didn't like where he'd put the back door off the kitchen. I also didn't like that he'd extended the opening between the foyer and the living room.

Who asked for that?

"I thought this is why we were meeting today. For *me* to

tell *you* what the house should look like. Why are there new plans with changes already?"

Calvin looked back over his shoulder. "This is the preliminary drawing based on what we talked about and a few ideas I had. Don't worry." He chuckled. "You still get the final say."

Good of him to remember that.

"First off, I don't want the foyer entrance into the living room changed at all." Reaching past him, I pointed to the back door. "And this needs to move. I want stairs that bypass the kitchen going straight up to the studio on the second floor, so there should be a door from the kitchen into the base of the stairwell on this corner over here."

"A studio?" he said.

"Yeah, that's where I'll do my engagement photos and portrait shoots."

Calvin rubbed his chin. "That changes things a bit."

His tone was not encouraging. "Changes them how?"

"Operating a business out of the house means getting different permits. I'm not sure that's possible in this residential area."

I had to have the studio. The renovations were going to take nearly all of my savings. After months of analyzing the budget from every angle, I'd figured out how I could survive, but there was no room for the added expense of an off-site studio.

"The studio is non-negotiable. I have to have it."

Calvin held up his hands. "I'm not saying you can't have it, but the zoning laws might. I need to check it out to see if it's possible."

Panic inched up my neck. Throughout my childhood,

different neighbors had run businesses out of the homes on Bammy's street. Mrs. Grooms sold cakes and pies out of her kitchen. Mrs. Carter had done tailoring and alterations, and even had three girls who worked for her with multiple machines set up in her den.

Had things changed so much in twenty years?

"It's not as if I'll be storing heavy equipment or making noise that could disturb the neighbors. I'm just taking pictures."

"That means bringing in clients," Calvin said, "which means additional traffic and cars parking on the street. Parking is a premium in this area, and residents don't want to have to compete with someone coming to get their picture taken for a spot in front of their own house."

He made it sound like I'd have a hundred people at once. "We're talking about maybe one car a few times a week, if that. I can leave the parking pad in the back for clients, then they won't be parking on the street at all."

"I'm not trying to argue with you," he said. "I'm just telling you how the zoning works, and why the rules are what they are. If we run into an issue, you'll have to take it up with the zoning board, but I can tell you, exceptions are rare."

Walter's words played back in my head. *It'll be a miracle if you get the permits needed.* I should have asked why he said that.

Panic would get me nowhere so I took a deep breath and tried to be positive. These were all maybes. A renovation project was always going to come with challenges. I hadn't planned on the challenge possibly hindering my business—

and my ability to pay the mortgage—but it wasn't as if I could turn back now.

Bammy's house was mine, and it was my job to bring it back to life. Whether that life would include a studio or not was a bridge I would cross on another day.

"Fine," I said with a nod. "The studio will remain a maybe, but the addition is a must either way. Let's move forward with the plans and deal with what exactly will go in the space above the kitchen at a later time."

The next ten minutes were spent discussing the first floor. Adding a few outlets. Expanding the size of the front window. Repairs to the fireplace and what materials I wanted. Bammy had once talked about how she hadn't wanted the red brick around the fire box, but Pops had insisted. That was enough for me to remove that brick without an ounce of regret.

The kitchen could have been a little more contentious, but in the end, Calvin's vision—though not what I'd originally imagined—made the room more functional with a clear flow. Torn between white cabinets and painted cabinets, we decided to leave that decision for another time as well. Determining the placement was enough for today.

Then we reached the second floor. That's where things got more heated.

"I have to have an ensuite on my bedroom."

"There's no pipes established in that area of the house."

"Then establish them."

"I'm a contractor, not a magician."

"What about over here?" Sheilah said, flipping the paper back to the first floor. "You're putting pipes here for the new powder room. Why not run them up the wall and take part of this bedroom for the new bath?"

Her suggestion put the bath on the opposite side from where I'd envisioned, but it also offered another opportunity I hadn't dared to dream of.

"Then we can use the other half of that bedroom for a walk-in closet." Hope alive once more, I grinned at the drawings, picturing my beautiful new closet with floor-to-ceiling shelves for my shoes and a special nook for purses. "It's perfect."

Reluctant to admit defeat, Calvin said, "You're willing to give up that bedroom? That'll leave you the small one across the hall for guests."

Everyone I knew lived here in town, so it wasn't as if I'd have company coming to stay.

"I'm fine with it."

He didn't look happy but he agreed to the change. Point for the kitchen to him. Point for the bathroom to me.

"Then we can do a walk-in shower for you and leave the tub in the hall bath."

Baths were not my thing, but there were times when a tub came in handy so I didn't argue.

By the end of the hour, Sheilah had a pad full of notes, and I was beyond pleased with the design. The hardest part would be waiting until it was finished and I could move in.

14 weeks wasn't a long time, but in this case felt like forever.

As we left the building, I said, "I can't believe I'll be in Bammy's house before Labor Day. You have no idea how much I'm looking forward to this."

"Labor Day?" Calvin said, stopping in place. "You need to aim more for Thanksgiving."

As soon as Calvin had agreed to do the job, I'd given notice on my loft. In four months I had to be out.

"Thanksgiving is too late," I said. "The renovation needs to be done by the end of August."

Running a hand over his face, he mumbled for a full twenty seconds before locking me with an incredulous stare. "It'll take at least three weeks for the permits alone. We can't break ground until those are in place. This is a neglected fifty-year-old house, bound to have issues we don't even know about yet. Finishing by the end of August is not going to happen."

"But everyone I talked to said the work would take four months." What the heck?

"The work, yes. But that's once we have the permits and the materials in place."

Crap. Why hadn't I double-checked before giving notice?

Leaning my butt against my car, I asked, "How much can you get done before Labor Day?"

His full lips pressed into a straight line. "Hard to tell until I start ordering supplies and get delivery dates."

There had to be a compromise. Even if the house wasn't finished, I could still live in it. They'd just have to work around me. I could be flexible, and even be absent when necessary.

"Start with the hall bath upstairs. If that's done, then I can move in and deal with the rest of the construction."

"Move in?" he repeated. The muscle in his jaw twitched. "You want to live *in the house* while we renovate it?"

I didn't *want* to, but I didn't have a choice.

"Lots of people do it, right?"

Calvin shook his head. "Not to this extent, and not in any job I've ever done."

Then this would be the proverbial first time for everything situation.

"I have to move into the house by the end of August. A working bathroom is all I'm asking for. I promise I'll stay out of the way until the job is done." Offering my brightest, and hopefully, most persuasive smile, I added, "You won't even know I'm there."

His snort was louder than necessary. "That's literally impossible." Conceding, he said, "It's your house. If you want to live in drywall dust and constant noise, that's your prerogative."

"Then you can have the bathroom done in time?"

"Can you meet me tomorrow to pick out the tile and vanity?"

I had three appointments and a rehearsal dinner to shoot. "I can give you an hour at noon."

"Fine." He pulled a wallet from his back pocket and passed me a card. "Meet me at this address at noon and be ready to make decisions. *Final* decisions."

Not a problem. "I'll be there."

———

"I can't decide," I muttered for the fourth time. Possibly the fifth.

The tiles were all so pretty. Did I want solid white, or

maybe go with black? I could choose black and white, but then there was that cream with the pretty blue swirl. Or the dusty rose swirl. No, that would be too feminine. Should they be installed vertical or horizontal? That affected the quantity so I had to know.

Why was this so hard?

Tina—the showroom designer and another long-time resident of Bammy's neighborhood—laughed while Calvin fought the urge to strangle me. We only had twenty minutes left before I had to get to my next appointment, which was adding pressure and making this task all the more difficult.

What if I get it wrong? What if once it was installed I hated it? As Calvin said, this needed to be a final decision. No changes. No takebacks. He would order the materials today so his team could start the install once they finished the demo.

To be fair, I *had* made decisions. The faucets, light fixtures, and the fancy toilet with a heated feature were all locked in. The tile, arguably the most important element in the entire room, was the only thing causing me trouble.

"I have an idea." Tina pulled a giant book from beneath the counter. "Let's see what style you gravitate toward."

The book was roughly the size of my coffee table, and as she opened the cover it felt like watching a witch open a giant book of spells. Maybe she had some magic that would get this job completed before I was forced to move in.

But then that would take a miracle, not witchcraft.

Tina pointed from the first page to the second. "This one leans a little more rustic, while this one is very clean and modern." She turned the page. "Then we have something a little more retro, which doesn't seem right for you at all." Another page flipped. "This is one of my favorites. A modern version of vintage without going too turn of the century. It's clean, but not too angular. The curves in the pattern really soften the entire look."

I was *in love*. The room was two-tone, with a muted green subway tile covering the bottom half of the walls, then going to the ceiling in the shower. The top third of the walls was white, while the floor featured a sweeping marble look, carrying similar green tones in the veining.

Not in a million years would I have guessed I'd go for a green bathroom, but the look was so perfect for the house. I could imagine Bammy choosing that tile, the floating light brown vanity, and even the muted brass drawer pulls.

"The light fixtures and faucets you've chosen would blend perfectly with this design," Tina assured me.

The hard sell was totally unnecessary.

"I'll take it."

"You'll what?" Calvin said, as if waking from a nap.

"This is the one," I said, pointing to the page. "This is my bathroom."

He leaned over my shoulder. "You want it up the walls like that?"

"Exactly as it is in the picture."

The lack of enthusiasm told me this would not have been his choice. Good thing he didn't have to live with it.

"The floor tile too?" he asked, making notes in his ever present notebook.

"Yes, and the vanity."

Leaning closer, he whistled. "That vanity is not in the budget."

"I can find you something similar at the right price," Tina assured. We hadn't been close friends back in the day, as she was nearly five years younger than me and we never ran in the same circles. But today Miss Tina Felton was quickly becoming my new favorite person.

"A friend of mine is considering buying a fixer-upper." Technically, Megan and Ryan had been too busy with wedding plans to start the house hunt in earnest, but that didn't stop her from sending links with 'Look at this one!' messages in the group chat. "I'm dragging her in here when they settle on something."

Her smile widened. "Thank you." Lowering her voice, she said, "A small discount is always an option when you refer a friend."

Calvin unfurled from the chair where he'd done little more than offer the occasional sigh at my indecision and handed Tina a sheet of paper. "Here's the dimensions of the room. Order whatever I need to create that picture, and put a rush on it if necessary."

"Consider it done."

After exchanging a low-key high five, I snagged one of Tina's business cards off the counter. "I'll be back when we get around to my new ensuite."

Dropping her guard a bit, Tina glanced around. "Thank you. We could use the business."

I also took in the room and noticed the lack of activity. In fact, Tina appeared to be the only employee on site.

Once Calvin and I were outside, I asked, "How long has this place been here?"

"Less than a year," he replied. "I'm their biggest customer, but one of their only customers. Are you really going to bring your friend?"

"Of course." I reached my car and checked the time. I still had ten minutes to grab a bite and make it to my next appointment. Thankfully, it wasn't far from here. "Why wouldn't I?" He was silent for so long I looked up to catch him staring at me as if I'd turned into a one-eyed alien. "What's that look about?"

"You keep surprising me."

He sounded more annoyed than pleased.

"Meaning I'm not the snob you thought I was?"

He ignored my question. "Just follow through, okay?"

"Follow through?"

"Tina was serious about needing the business. Don't say you'll bring someone, and then not do it."

Amazing. No matter what I did, he continued to think the worst of me.

"I have someplace to be." Climbing into the car, I dropped my junk on the passenger seat and buckled up, putting the annoying contractor out of my mind.

Chapter Five

C ALVIN WOULD NOT GET OUT OF MY HEAD. H IS assumptions were starting to hurt, which annoyed me even more. He and I had never been the best of friends, but I'd never acted too good for anyone. During the summer months, I'd practically lived with Bammy, and that had made me part of the neighborhood. The kids on that block were my friends. Maybe I should have done more to stay in touch, but we all grew up and moved on.

Or so I'd thought.

Right on time, I rushed into the hotel where I was meeting Becca and her clients. They were looking at this location and wanted advice on where they could capture the perfect images if this became their final choice.

Located in Station Square, the venue sat right on the river directly across from downtown, offering an amazing view across the water. The back wall of the bar area and the event room off of it were floor to ceiling glass to make the most of this feature.

That event room was where I found Becca and the happy couple. Brad and Wendy were young, beautiful, and madly in love. A hotel rep was pitching the space when I tapped Becca on the shoulder. "Hey," I whispered when she turned my way.

"Hey," she whispered back. Her eyes lacked their normal glow, and her cheeks, though rounder than ever, seemed pale.

At a pause in the sales pitch, Becca brought me into the conversation, introducing me to the hotel rep as Wendy gave me a hug in greeting. The bride-to-be then peppered me with questions and I made my recommendations, suggesting we head outside so I could show her potential picture locations for the big day. I took a couple using her phone, and she bounced with excitement when she saw how perfect the setting was.

When the hotel rep took them upstairs to see the guest rooms, Becca and I settled at a table in the bar.

"Are you okay?" I asked. Not that I expected a woman about to give birth to be full of energy, but the circles under her eyes were concerning.

With a sigh, she shrugged. "As good as I can be. The doctor says the baby is healthy, and that's what matters, but I'd give anything for a full night's sleep."

Becca had a tendency to put herself last more than she should so as not to let anyone down. Back around the time she met Jacob, her boss had taken medical leave to deal with cancer, dropping the whole business in Becca's lap. Toward the end of that week she'd fainted in the middle of a busy restaurant from stretching herself too thin. Thankfully, Jacob had been there to catch her.

"Maybe you should start your leave now. We need the baby *and* you to be healthy."

"Amanda suggested that, but it's not as if my job is strenuous. Besides, what would I do? Sit around twiddling my thumbs waiting for my water to break? Or for the doc to make the call early?"

"Yes," I said. "That's exactly what you should do. It's not as if you'll get any sleep once the baby is here, so you might as well take the time to rest now. Especially if your boss is telling you to go home."

"Now you sound like Lindsey."

"We're just worried about you, hon. What does Jacob say?"

Her phone dinged and she checked the screen, then turned it my way. "He's texting me twice an hour to see how I'm feeling." The little box in the middle of the screen showed his name and the message *Are you feeling okay?* "He agrees with the rest of you," she said, "but is leaving the decision up to me."

She really was the most stubborn person I knew. Which was saying something considering most people thought *I* was the most stubborn person *they* knew.

Going for a compromise, I said, "What about taking half days? You'd still be working, just fewer hours."

"That isn't a bad idea," she said while typing her husband a response. "The new planner Amanda hired over the winter is doing really well. She could probably take some of my appointments."

"There you go."

"And I would love to go home and take an afternoon nap."

This was becoming an easier sell by the second. "You should do it. Do you have any more appointments today?"

She hit send and set the phone on the table. "I did but they cancelled this morning. A sweet woman wanted to discuss a retirement party for her mom, but the company got bought out, and then let her go before she could retire. Can you believe that?"

Thank goodness I was self-employed. "Wow. That's awful."

"I know." Leaning back and rubbing her belly, she said, "Enough about me. Did you find a contractor yet?"

With all the baby talk, I'd forgotten to update the group chat. "I did. A guy from Bammy's neighborhood. We knew each other when we were kids, and now he flips houses in the area."

"Donna, that's great. Will the work begin right away? When will you get to move in?"

"That's a bit of an issue."

"What?" She scooted back in her chair, trying to sit up straighter. "Why?"

Because I was an idiot, that was why. "Once I locked in the contractor, I gave notice on my apartment. Then I found out the job will take longer than I thought. I called the building manager to change my move-out date, but because there's a waiting list to get into the building, she'd already promised the apartment to someone else."

"Can't she *un*promise it?"

I wished. "Nope. The lease is signed."

A waitress swung by to fill our water glasses. "What are you going to do?" Becca asked before offering a "Thank you" to the server.

"The only thing I can do. I'll have to move into the house while it's still being renovated."

Her eyes went wide. "Can you do that?"

"Calvin promised me I'd have a working bathroom, which is all I really need. The main bedroom will get new floors, then I'll do the painting myself, since it would cost extra to make the house painter come in early to do only one room."

"Calvin is the contractor?"

"Yeah, Calvin Hopkins. He isn't happy about me moving in, but there's no other choice so he'll have to deal with it."

"You can always come stay with us," she offered, clearly forgetting that their apartment was about to get quite crowded.

"You're already getting a new little roommate. The last thing you need is me underfoot."

"I'm sure one of the other girls will be happy to let you stay."

They would. But Josie had Miles and Megan had Ryan, plus house hunting and wedding planning, and Lindsey was unapologetically messy. I wouldn't make it one night without having to scour her house, and she'd have it just as messy within days.

There was also the fact that I was fiercely independent and saw no need to intrude on my friends when I had a whole house of my own. Would said house be in a livable condition? Debatable. But a roof over my head and a working bathroom would be enough, at least temporarily.

Also, I was looking forward to being in the middle of the project. Rationally, I knew I didn't have the skills to do the physical labor, but I still needed to feel like I was part of the process. Like I could contribute more than pointing at a picture and saying, "I like that one."

"I appreciate the thought, but I'll be fine. It'll be fun to have a front row seat to watch the place come together." I'd remind myself of this the first time some dude in a tool belt caught me in my bathrobe. "If all goes well, we'll have a Friendsgiving dinner in my beautiful new home come November."

This was my dream. To gather friends and family and bring life back to Bammy's house. She had loved to entertain. Her greatest joy, other than her grandchildren, was to cook for anyone and everyone. My greens would never be as good as hers, but she'd been a patient teacher, and I still remembered most of the recipes that had been stored in her memory but never written down.

The summer after she passed, I put as many as I could into a notebook and intended to turn them into a family cookbook, but never got that far. Another Bammy project I needed to complete.

The couple returned with the hotel rep and Wendy was still bouncing. "This is it," she said. "This is where we want to get married."

Becca displayed all the enthusiasm she could manage. "Okay, then." She turned to the rep. "You heard the bride. Lock us in for next June."

I whipped out my phone to update the information in my calendar. "Still the second Saturday?" I asked.

"Yes." The bride spun and gave her groom a quick kiss. "This is going to be everything we imagined."

He chuckled. "I'm just glad we can mark venue off the list." Nodding to Becca, he said, "When do we get to do the cake tasting? That's what I'm looking forward to."

She pushed her chair back and I helped her reach her feet. If I hadn't been so close, I might have missed the muffled hiss that crossed her lips.

Rubbing her side, Becca smiled. "I can set that up for next week if you want. Let me check my calendar and give you a call to pick a time."

Considering the lack of color in her cheeks and the way she looked ready to drop back into the chair, I had a funny feeling another event planner would be handling the taste test.

"Great." The groom-to-be kissed his fiancée's forehead. "I need to get back to work, and I know you're dying to call the moms and tell them about this place."

"Don't forget about dinner at Mike and Margo's," she said as he hurried away. With a wave of acknowledgement, he disappeared around the corner and she turned to Becca. "Are you okay?"

"Of course," Becca said. "Do you want to discuss the day more in detail, or save that for another time?"

Wendy leaned in and patted Becca's hand. "We have over a year to deal with all of that. I'm more worried about you. If we need to do the cake thing after you're back from maternity leave, that's totally fine."

Some people assumed that in mine and Becca's line of work, we spent most of our time with selfish, demanding bridezillas, but there were far more clients like Wendy than the other. Caring and patient and great to work with.

Making a rare concession, Becca said, "I am a bit tired. But we have another planner in the office who can handle the tasting. You won't have to put the planning on hold for me, I promise."

Chestnut hair swayed as the bride-to-be shook her head. "No need for a new planner. I'm totally happy to wait. Besides, giving birth is much more important than planning a wedding. You're literally growing a human. I'm just throwing a party." Her laughter filled the air and I could have hugged her. "Just be sure to send me lots of pictures once the little guy is here. I'm in no hurry to have my own, but I love the ones I can coo over, then give back."

My preferred baby encounters as well. Though I might make an exception for baby Noah. We'd all threatened to kidnapped him at one point or another. Not that Jacob would let us get far if we did. I'd never seen a happier expectant father in my life.

"I'm sure there will be days when I'm toting him around so I'll make sure you get to meet him. If he doesn't make his appearance soon, I'm afraid by body might go on strike. My bladder for sure." With another hiss, Becca bent over and braced her hands on the table.

"Are you okay?" I asked, ready to catch her if she went down.

She nodded and reached back for the chair. Wendy and I stood on each side helping her ease onto the seat. "I'm convinced this child is going to be a star soccer player the way he kicks. Pretty sure that one was a kidney."

Wendy slid Becca's water glass closer. "Maybe you should drink something. Are you sure it was just a kick?" Looking at me, she asked, "Does this happen a lot?"

That's when I realized I hadn't seen Becca much lately, because I had no idea.

"A lot in the last week," Becca said, shifting in the chair as if trying to get comfortable. That ship had clearly sailed. "If I eat something and put my feet up for a while, he should relax again."

Gathering Becca's things, I said to Wendy, "I'm going to pull my car up to the entrance. Can you get her out there so I can take her home?"

"Of course."

"I don't want—" Becca started.

"No arguments, woman. You're going home for the rest of the day. We'll call Amanda and let her know." Grabbing her purse, I slung both hers and mine over my shoulder. "I'm also calling Jacob so he knows what's going on."

She moaned. "If you tell him then he won't let me move again until the baby is here."

"That sounds like the right plan to me," Wendy said.

While Becca pouted, I gave the younger woman an appreciative hug. "Thank you for your help, and for being so cool about the planning stuff."

She waved my words away. "My cousin got married last year and was a complete nightmare about the whole thing. Then her husband moved out within three months of the wedding. Put things in perspective real quick."

This. This is what I kept saying. What came *after* the wedding was so much more important than having the most expensive dress or the most lavish flowers.

Minutes later, Becca was in the car and we headed for the interstate. I made calls to both Amanda and Jacob along the way, while my passenger pouted that this was all unnecessary and that women had babies every day and that she was fine.

I ignored her while dialing up her mother. If anyone could make Becca stay on the couch for the rest of the day, it was Kathy Witherspoon.

———

"How ARE we supposed to have a Sunday dinner without Mama's potato salad?" Dad asked for the third time since I'd arrived empty-handed.

I repeated the same answer I'd given the first two times. "There was no time after the wedding yesterday. You'll have it next time."

He huffed, mostly to get under my skin. Dad was nothing if not an agitator.

As usual, Mom put out the full spread. Placemats, centerpiece, and the gold-trimmed plates. The settings were tasteful and understated for a formal gathering, but overkill for a casual family dinner.

"You had a wedding yesterday?" Mom asked.

"An evening one, yeah, but we started pictures in the afternoon."

"Then you had all morning to make the salad," Dad

pointed out as Mom set the last bowl on the table and took her seat across from me. Her smooth hair pulled back in a clip showed off the burnt-orange tassel earrings that accentuated her long, slender neck.

I wish I could say I looked just like her, but that was not the case. Sadly. I inherited my looks from Dad's side of the family, all curves and rounded edges, whereas Mom was more straight lines and elegance.

"Decisions needed to be made about the renovation so I was out most of the day."

Calvin sent a text Saturday morning saying the flooring I'd picked was on backorder with no known delivery date. I could wait, which would push back getting my room done in time for me to move in, or I could choose a different floor. Since waiting wasn't an option, I met him at the flooring place to make a new selection.

I'd be living with these floors for the rest of my life, so I wasn't about to make a decision without considering all of the options. The slightest change in finish could look too orange in one light or too gray in another, and my first three selections were dismissed because they would also end up on backorder.

After that, Calvin made the salesperson—who happened to be another local from Bammy's neighborhood—show us only the options we could get immediately. Thankfully, I fell in love with the second one he brought out, but that was more than an hour into the process. By the time we discussed paint colors, finishes, and more affordable replacements for some of the bathroom design, my morning was shot.

"I still can't believe you bought that old, rundown house," Mom said. "What were you thinking?"

"The house just needs a little work," I said, ignoring the second part. We'd been through this before. Dad grew up in the house and, at times, seemed to get my attachment to it, but Mom never understood.

Face twisted in distaste, she said, "It's so small."

The home we were in—a sturdy three story in Dormont with large rooms, high ceilings, and a sizeable lot—was not the house I grew up in. It wasn't until I was in high school that my parents were able to upgrade from the tiny, two-bedroom apartment in East Liberty—the part of town where Mom grew up—to this house. I'd spent less than a year here before going off to college.

"Small was good enough for us," I reminded her. "And I'm adding on so there will more square footage when it's done."

Dad spooned a mound of mashed potatoes onto his plate. "Adding on? That sounds expensive."

The addition took up a large chunk of the budget, but would be worth the expense when I had my dream kitchen, and hopefully a new studio.

"Calvin has assured me that everything I want to do is possible within my budget."

"Calvin?" Mom said. "Calvin who?"

I took the bowl of potatoes Dad passed my way. "Calvin Hopkins. He's from the neighborhood and is the contractor on the project."

"Evie Hopkins' boy?" Dad asked. "Didn't he always have a crush on you?"

"Really?" Mom said, suddenly more interested in the topic.

That I remained unmarried and without a family of my own was her greatest disappointment. A fact she stated repeatedly. You'd think she'd be proud that her daughter built a business out of nothing, but no.

I kept filling my plate. "No, he didn't. In fact, we barely tolerated each other, but he's the only contractor I could find willing to take the job."

Dad shook his head. "Bammy said he used to come around asking for you all the time. Wanted to know when you were coming back for a stay. That boy liked you."

I doubted that was the case.

"Is he from a good family?" Mom asked.

"Evie had her struggles." Dad added a pile of greens next to his potatoes. "Last I heard, he was flipping a lot of the houses over that way. Bringing the neighborhood back to what it used to be. I suppose you could do worse than that boy."

"He's just my contractor," I reiterated. "We don't even like each other."

"He's single then?" Mom passed a roll to Dad before sliding the butter his way. "Is he handsome?"

Because I was a terrible liar, I said, "Yes, he's handsome. If you like the hammer-swinging, overall-wearing type."

Rolling straight into her plotting ways, Mom rubbed her hands together like an evil villain with a victim in her sights. "That sounds like husband material to me. Lord, give me a capable man any day."

I expected Dad to take offense, since he could barely

change a light bulb let alone replace a light fixture, but he was grinning my way. "You'll need to spend a lot of time together for the next few months. Couldn't hurt to see where things go."

These two were delusional.

"It's going to lead to Bammy's house being renovated and me living in it *alone*. I will not be trying to turn Calvin, or any other man, into my husband, thank you very much. You guys need to let this go."

"Why?" Mom asked, sounding hurt. "Why would getting married be so awful? Your Dad and I have been together since we were fifteen years old, and I wouldn't change a single minute."

Their marriage wasn't perfect, and I knew for a fact that last claim wasn't true. Not only had she broken up with Dad twice before they'd graduated high school, but she'd almost called off the wedding three times. Then there'd been that summer when Dad had stayed at Bammy's for more than a month because Mom had kicked him out.

She wasn't fooling anyone. Happily ever after was rare and never a smooth ride.

"I never said getting married would be awful. It just isn't for me. I like my independence, and I have yet to meet a man who would actually make my life easier instead of harder. Men are needy and looking for mothers not wives. I'd rather stay single than deal with all that."

Silence fell over the table as I scooped up a spoonful of etouffee. Mom's family had moved up from southern Louisiana, and brought the region's traditional dishes with them.

"That's a bit harsh," Dad finally said.

I glanced up when Mom stayed silent, and the look on her face said it all. I loved my dad, and he'd been a great father, but there were plenty of times when she probably felt as if she had two kids instead of one.

"When will the place be ready for you to move in?" she asked, dropping the husband subject.

"I'm moving in at the end of August, but the work won't be done until around Halloween."

"You're moving in before it's finished?" Dad asked.

Reaching for a roll, I nodded. "I have to. I thought the job would be done sooner so I gave notice on my apartment, then they gave it to someone else before I could ask for an extension."

"You'll be living in a construction zone," Mom said. "I don't know why you have to live there at all. Why don't you rent that one out, and buy a house over here? There's a cute one for sale two blocks down. Think of how nice it would be to live so close."

Nice was not the word that came to mind. But also, how did she think I could afford to buy multiple houses? It took ten years to save up enough for the first one.

"I'm not renting out Bammy's house. That's *my* house. *I'm* going to live in it. The construction won't last long, and then I'll have exactly what I want in the place where I have the best memories."

Mom and Dad exchanged a glance, hurt obvious in their expressions. I didn't mean to hurt them. Things just were what they were. They'd both worked. I'd been alone. A lot. There had been...issues. No one is perfect and I didn't hold a grudge, but Bammy's is where I was happy. Where I wasn't alone.

"I'm sure it's going to be real nice," Dad said with a gentle smile. "Can't wait to see it."

I nodded. "Me, too."

Mom kept her eyes on her plate and stayed silent.

Chapter Six

Four days later, I found myself walking through my muddy backyard, debating exactly how far out my new addition should go. Calvin could tell me what the square footage would be at each spot, but getting an accurate picture in my mind wasn't happening.

"So if we go to here," I said, walking to the middle line spray painted on the dirt, "how big would the kitchen be?"

He checked his trusty notebook. "Two hundred twenty-eight square feet. If we go to the last line, you'll get two hundred fifty."

I walked to the last line and looked back at the house. "That isn't helping me."

Calvin stepped up next to me. "Imagine all of this space, plus the nine feet you have inside. All of that together is how big the kitchen will be."

He smelled really good.

Focus, Donna. Focus.

Spinning to face the alley, I asked, "Then how far out will the back porch have to go?"

"How far do you want it to go?"

I hated when he answered my question with a question.

"Isn't there a standard porch size?"

"Not in this case, no."

Funny how karma had a way of swinging around and biting you on the butt. I wanted to make all of the decisions, but I clearly hadn't thought this through.

Taking several large steps toward the alley, I said, "How big is this?"

Calvin whipped out his tape measure and without bending down, dropped it the length that I'd covered. "Just over four feet."

Eyeing the distance to the garage, I asked, "How long is the garage again?"

"Fifteen feet."

"Then the porch could go back farther since we're taking out the one side, right?"

"Yes, ma'am."

Cutting him a dry look, I crossed my arms. "Ma'am?"

"We're doing good," he said. "Don't pick a fight over nothing."

"Is that what you think I do? Pick fights?"

He nodded.

"So I'm stuck up *and* contentious." As if pleading the fifth, he stayed silent. "That's a little pot meets kettle, isn't it?"

Brown eyes widened as the tape measure snapped back into its case. "Are you saying I'm stuck up and contentious?"

"Yes."

For a split second, a smile danced across his lips and my heart did an unexpected flip. Turning back to the house, he said, "You see? Always picking fights."

"We wouldn't fight if you didn't poke at me." I followed him into the kitchen. "You're the instigator."

"Poke at you? You get mad if I just enter the room. It's always been that way."

"What way?"

He hooked the tape measure on a loop on his hip and tucked the notebook into his front pocket. "You never liked me. Even when we were kids."

That wasn't remotely true. "*You* never liked *me*."

Brow furrowed, he said, "I liked you more than I should have. You broke my heart back in middle school."

"Now you're making stuff up." I crossed to the counter and leaned against it. "I never broke your heart." If anything, he broke mine. Not that I would be confessing to that.

Calvin snorted. "Whenever I wanted to go down to the convenience store, you'd push back and want to get ice cream at Sylvester's."

A serious twist of the truth. "You were the one who pushed back any time I made a suggestion. Why would we go all the way down to that store when Sylvester's was right on the corner?"

"Because I wanted to spend more time with you."

The words hung in the air as I stared in confusion, unable to process what he'd said.

"*You* wanted to spend more time with *me*?" I asked.

"Why else would I have picked the place farther away?"

I went with the obvious choice. "To be a jerk? To be the one calling the shots instead of me, the outsider?"

His gaze locked on mine. "That's what you thought?"

"What else was I supposed to think? You hardly ever talked to me, and when you did it was to contradict anything I said."

"I was fourteen and had a huge crush on you. I didn't talk to you because when you were around my mind went blank. All I could think about was how pretty you were." Strong arms crossed over a broad chest, testing the stitching on his T-shirt sleeves. "You had it all wrong. I never hated you, Donna. Far from it."

Stunned, I struggled to wrap my brain around this revelation. How could I have known. He was a young teen with his first crush, but so was I.

"I had no idea."

"Was I ever outright mean to you?" he asked.

Thinking back, countless encounters raced through my mind. "You never called me names, if that's what you mean. But you always made me feel unwelcome. Like no one should listen to me because I wasn't really a part of the neighborhood."

His expression softened. "That's what you thought?"

"That's how I felt."

Calvin ran a hand over his face. "Man, I'm sorry. That was never my intention."

My whole body relaxed, as if hearing his apology drained the anxiety I carried into all of our encounters. "I'm sorry, too. I might have been a little too defensive and assumed the worst about you."

One side of his mouth curled in a half grin. "Might have?"

"We're doing well here. Don't start poking."

Nodding, he took a step forward. "That wasn't poking. That was teasing."

Heat danced up my spine at his tone, and I wasn't sure how to handle this new vibe between us. I'd seen him as the enemy for so long, seeing him as anything else was going to take time.

"We've cleared up the past," I said. "How about the present?"

"What about the present?"

"Do you still see me as stuck up?" Regret set in when he took too long to answer. "Forget it." I moved to walk past him. "Let's just do this job and go our separate ways."

A strong hand wrapped around my arm, stopping me in place. There was no pressure or anger. Just a gentle touch that sent heat racing through my bloodstream.

"I was wrong, okay? How about we start over?"

Inches apart, I stared into his eyes, worried this might be a joke. A way to disarm me, and then tell me none of this was true.

"Truce?" he said, genuine sincerity in his voice.

Relaxing, I nodded. "Truce."

———

AFTER WE AGREED to the truce, Calvin stepped outside to take a phone call, giving me time to process these new revelations. So he hadn't hated me after all. Huh. I wasn't sure how to feel about this. That angsty, heartbroken teen still lived deep in my psyche, and she was torn between feeling like an idiot and being angry that he never freaking said something.

Not sure what to do with the past, I focused on the present. This didn't change anything between us. We were kids back then. Clueless kids, obviously, but that was a long time ago. We were adults now. Different people entirely. I hadn't thought about Calvin in years, and he likely never thought of me either.

Childhood crushes were meant to be left in the past. So why was my only thought about what could have been?

"Sorry about that," Calvin said, stepping into the kitchen. "We're wrapping up a job over on Terrace and the fridge got ordered in the wrong size."

"Do you handle every detail like that?" I was a one-woman show in my business, but I assumed he had a full staff.

"Mostly." He slid the phone into his pocket. "I like to keep things simple. The less people between me and the work, the better."

Not a bad approach. After ten years of wearing all the hats, I was considering hiring a part-time assistant to take calls, book appointments, and give me a little more time for the creative side. Editing photos was by far my favorite thing to do, but the more clients booked meant having to push that part into my evenings.

A catch twenty-two of sorts. More clients equaled more money, but also less time for having a life.

"Are you ever off the clock?" I asked.

His hands slipped into his pockets. "I make time for things when I need to."

I laughed. "In other words, no."

This was the first time we'd talked without animosity getting in the way. It felt good. Besides Josie, I didn't get much time with other small business owners. Self-starters who built something out of nothing. Josie's bookkeeping business wasn't a creative endeavor, so though there were similarities, we weren't quite the same.

The fine line between art and commerce is where I spent most of my days. Flipping houses was likely similar.

"Do you ever clock out from the photography thing?" he asked. "Other than when you're here, anyway."

Now that he mentioned it, this house was the only part of my life that didn't revolve around the business. This and the girls, and I didn't spend nearly as much time with them as I'd like.

"I do Sunday dinners with Mom and Dad, and my friends and I meet for breakfast once or twice a month." I couldn't come up with anything else. "Maybe I do work a little too much."

"What do you do to blow off steam?"

The question did not compute. "What do you mean?"

Calvin leaned back against the wall. "You know. Something to relieve stress."

Looking at him, all relaxed and casually sexy, only one form of stress relief came to mind, and we were not doing *that*.

Examining one of the broken cabinet doors, I said,

"Nothing I can think of." Because I couldn't help myself, I asked, "What do you do?"

"I break things," he replied.

"I'm sorry, what?"

Deep laughter filled the room and did nothing to clean up the thoughts in my brain. "It's called demolition. One of the perks of renovations is that you get to break things before you rebuild them." Nodding toward the counter, he added, "You should try it."

My eyes went to the counter, and then back to Calvin. "I should try *breaking things?*"

I understood that what was here had to go, but that should be left to professionals, shouldn't it?

"Sure." He closed the space between us and reached down past the end of the counter. "With this." Calvin picked up the largest hammer I'd ever seen.

"With *that?* It doesn't even look like I could lift it."

Professional cameras were heavy, and I'd been hefting one kind or another around for more than a decade. But this hammer looked like something only Thor could lift.

Calvin flipped it with one hand and extended the handle in my direction. Quite possibly the sexiest move I'd ever seen *in my life*. "Go for it. Take out the counter."

Was I really going to do this? Backing down had never been my thing, but neither was destroying kitchen counters.

"Am I qualified to do this? I assume you have a team of trained professionals."

Patiently holding the hammer in the air, he said, "You think a person has to go to school to learn how to break a counter?" I supposed one stupid question deserved another.

"There are things here I won't let you get near, but I know the water is off, so the worst you can do is give yourself a splinter. Or maybe you're afraid of breaking a nail?"

That was definitely a poke.

I held up my hands. "Do you see any fancy nails here?" In truth, I loved getting my nails done, but they interfered with my work so short stubby nails it had to be.

His grin widened. "Then take the hammer." Whipping a pair of clear glasses from some back pocket, he extended them as well. "Safety first."

Where did... "Are those magical overalls? Where the heck do you keep all this stuff?"

"Pockets." The hammer head hit the floor and he leaned the tool my way. "Swing it straight up, and let the weight bring it down on the counter."

He made it sound so easy. After sliding on the glasses, I grabbed the hammer with both hands and took a step back from the counter while Calvin shuffled into the living room, giving me plenty of room to swing.

Focusing on where I wanted the thing to land, I took a deep breath, then pulled back, swinging the hammer in a full circle until it came crashing down in the middle of the counter. The corner shot across the room, and the rest of it detached from the wall. Only the far end was holding it up.

"Hit it again," Calvin urged.

Energy from the first hit was still reverberating up my arms, but I followed the order. This time the hammer smashed into the sink, jerking the cabinets the rest of the way off the wall.

The mess tumbled forward, and I hopped back with a

squeal. Not my most girl power moment, but what an adrenaline rush.

Let's do that again.

"What about the top ones?" I asked. "They have to come down, too, right?"

A proud smile split his far-too-attractive face. "Yes, ma'am."

This was going to take a bit more finesse since I couldn't drop the hammer straight down. That didn't mean I couldn't use gravity in my favor, but I preferred to do so without dislocating a shoulder.

I could see me trying to explain the injury. *Calvin was looking all hot and he dared me to break something so I did and I ended up breaking myself.*

The girls would never let me live it down.

Deciding to go side arm instead of overhead, I turned and squared up around the fallen debris on the floor. Grip tight, I reared back and swung the hammer straight into the center door of the upper cabinets. Wood splintered everywhere and I held an arm over my face by instinct. Unfortunately, this meant letting go of the hammer, which landed with a thud on the top of my foot.

This time, gravity was *not* in my favor,

Holding back a slew of very bad words, which Bammy never would have tolerated in her house, I hopped around until my butt hit the wall, and then I slid to the floor. Before my bottom met linoleum, Calvin was by my side.

"Take deep breaths and let me check it out." His calm voice didn't help the pain, but it did ease the pending hysteria.

Please don't let it be broken. Please don't let it be broken.

"Ouch," I yelled when he pressed on the foot. "Holy crap, that hurts."

"We need to get the boot off before it swells. Are you good with me doing that?"

These were my favorite knee-high boots so I did *not* want to have to cut them off.

I nodded. "I'm good. Just pull it."

Teeth clenched, I closed my eyes and held my breath as leather brushed over where the hammer had landed. Not until my foot was free could I fill my lungs again.

Peeking out one eye, I asked, "How bad is it?"

"It's already swelling. We need to get some ice on it."

I didn't exactly have a working freezer in the house. "Where are we going to get that?"

"My place." He rose to his feet and extended both hands. "Grab hold." Without thought, I put my hands in his and was hoisted upright as if I weighed no more than a child. "Can you walk?" he asked.

I put weight on my foot and saw stars. "Nope. No walking."

"Then I'll have to carry you."

That snapped me back to my senses. "You live two blocks away."

"So?"

There was macho, and then there was crazy. "You aren't carrying me two blocks. We can drive my car over. My keys are in the foyer."

"You're right. That's a better idea."

Of course, it was. Thankfully, my left foot was the

injured one, so I could still drive. Calvin retrieved my keys and before I could take them they disappeared into one of his magical pockets with a jingle.

"Put your weight on me," he said, bending a bit.

I draped my left arm across his shoulders, and he tucked a hand up under my right armpit. We were doing well until we reached the side door and there was no way both of us would fit at the same time.

"We'll have to go one at a time." He untangled us—never completely letting go—stepped out backwards, and before I knew it, swung me down to the ground. "Can you make it to the car?"

A tiny voice in my brain said *let him carry you*, but thankfully, my pride told that voice to shut the heck up.

"I can do it. Just keep me upright."

It wasn't the most graceful trip across the yard, but we made it. I was so focused on not falling or dropping my foot that I failed to notice him leading me to the passenger side of the car.

"What are you doing?"

"Putting you in the car."

"But the driver's seat is over there."

Calvin pressed the button on the key fob. "Letting me drive your car for two blocks isn't going to kill you."

Loretta, as I called her, was an older model coupe and had a mind of her own. "She's finicky," I said.

Brows arched high. "More than you are?"

So much for the truce. "I can go home and get my own ice."

He stepped back. "You could, but how are you going to get from the car to your apartment?"

Good question. This accepting help thing wasn't easy.

"When you come to a stop sign, you have to put her in neutral and give her a little gas or she'll stall."

Calvin bent to look inside the car. "Is it a manual?"

Head high, I said, "No."

Opening the car door, he maneuvered me into the passenger seat, then rested an arm above my head and bent until we were almost eye to eye. "At some point, we're going to discuss getting you a new car."

"My car is fine."

"Dying at stop signs is not fine."

Jaw tight, I mumbled, "I can't afford a new car."

Every single penny I'd scraped together was going into the house. The months of the renovation were my busiest, and that would bring in more income, but not enough to replace Loretta. Not yet.

Without another word, Calvin closed the door.

Chapter Seven

Calvin lived in the house he grew up in, so I'd been there before, but I expected it to look completely different. Instead, it looked exactly the same.

We made the two block drive in silence, because all I could concentrate on was the pain throbbing through my foot. I also didn't want to discuss my car. Rationally, I knew there was nothing to be embarrassed about. We all chose our priorities and mine was the house. But I portrayed this image of an independent woman with her crap together, and Loretta trying to stall every chance she got did not fit that picture.

Thankfully, my business didn't require driving clients around. Loretta looked perfectly respectable on the outside. Her flaws were of the under-the-hood variety. And in my defense, I planned to put her in the shop as soon as I could afford a rental.

If the dying car wasn't enough, the trip from the car to the house was just as humbling. With luck, no one saw me hobbling on one foot, one boot missing and clinging to Calvin for dear life. If rumors popped up about him dragging a drunk woman into his house in the middle of the day, I wouldn't be surprised.

Sitting on the floral sofa where he left me, I debated how to ask why his house looked untouched since the eighties. I had hired this man to flip my house, but this setting was not filling me with confidence that I'd made the right choice.

"You can put your foot up on the coffee table," he said, returning from the kitchen with a bag of frozen peas and a tea towel. After gently laying the towel across my foot, he placed the bag of peas on top of it. I braced for the pain, but only felt the cold. "Is that good?" he asked.

I nodded. "Yeah." Calvin took a seat in one of the wing-back chairs on the opposite side of the coffee table, and I tested my extremities. "It doesn't hurt as much when I move my toes."

"That's good. Hopefully, the hammer didn't land straight on."

"I don't know. That really hurt."

"I'm sorry," he said.

"For what?" I was the one who dropped the thing.

"I never should have let you demo the counter. Not without the proper gear."

He looked so contrite I felt the need to lighten the mood. "I had glasses on, remember?"

His expression remained apologetic. "You need work boots for stuff like that. I should have known better. If you need to see a doc for this, I'll pay the bill."

I appreciated the offer, but there was no need. "Calvin,

I'm a grown woman. I took the hammer, and I should have held onto it. Stop beating yourself up. Accidents happen."

"In my line of work, accidents can cost lives."

Okay, he had me there. "I'm still alive," I assured him. "Besides, breaking that counter might be the most fun I've had in months. If I get the right gear, can I help break more stuff?"

Calvin smiled for the first time since my initial yowl of pain. "You want to help with demo?"

"If it's a day I'm free, yeah. That was a serious adrenaline rush." Grin in place, he watched me in silence. "What?" I asked.

"You keep surprising me."

The softness in his tone did uncomfortable things to my peace of mind. Going for deflection, I said, "Can I ask you something?"

Rich brown eyes dropped to the hands in his lap. "Ask away."

"Don't take this the wrong way, but why does this house look the same as when we were kids? Shouldn't a house flipper's house be the best looking house on the block?"

He assessed our surroundings. "Well, for one, I flip houses not just to improve the neighborhood, but to make money. Putting hours, funds, and sweat into this place just for me is pointless."

"That's fair, but since you said *for one*, there must be another reason."

Calvin pressed his head back against the chair. "I guess you could say I prefer not to disturb the ghosts."

He had my attention. "The ghosts?"

"Why do you want to live in your Bammy's house so badly?" he asked, the change of topic catching me off guard.

"Because that's where my best memories were made. Bammy's house was my safe place, and I want to bring life to it again."

With sadness in his eyes, he nodded. "That wasn't the case here."

My heart went out to the boy I knew. On summer days our group would sometimes stop at random houses for snacks or drinks, but now that I thought about it, we never came here. In all those years, I'd maybe been in the Hopkins house two or three times, and we were never invited in beyond the foyer.

"I'm sorry. I had no idea."

"Not many did. It's not like anyone could have done much about it." Shifting to the edge of his seat, he nodded toward my foot. "How's it feel?"

I wiggled my toes. "Numb mostly. The throbbing went away."

"That's a good sign." Moving to the couch beside me, he lifted the towel and peas away. "Looks like the swelling has gone down. You want to try putting weight on it?"

Being off my feet for any period of time would mean lost income, so I needed this to be superficial at best. Nothing more than a bruise at worst.

"Let me try." Lowering my foot to the floor, I pressed a bit to test it. Definitely a twinge, but not the shooting pain from earlier. Pushing off the couch, I rose to my feet, keeping most of the weight on my right foot. After a deep breath, I shifted more weight to the injured one and found the pain tolerable. "It isn't too bad."

"You haven't walked on it yet." Standing, he offered his hand. "Hold on just in case."

Our fingers intertwined and the warmth of his palm pressed against mine. The heat extended to other parts of my body, making walking on my own an immediate necessity.

Taking a few shaky steps, the pain definitely increased, but nothing I couldn't handle. Plus, keeping most of the weight on my heel would work until the rest of the foot was better.

"I'm okay," I said, When I dropped his hand I lost my balance, and Calvin braced strong hands on my hips to keep me steady. I practically jumped away from him. "I'm good. Really. Look." I hobbled with the grace of a drunk ostrich. "It's fine."

"You nearly took out my coffee table. Just take it slow."

So he was more worried about his furniture than about me. That was good.

"The unevenness of wearing one shoe threw me off, that's all. I just need my other boot."

"We left that back at the other house."

I lamented limping back in my sock before remembering there were shoes in my car. "There's a pair of sneakers behind the passenger seat in my car. I can change into those."

Before I could take two steps toward the door, Calvin cut me off. "Can you chill, please? I'll get the shoes."

He mumbled something under his breath as he walked away and since I doubted it was positive, I pretended not to hear. Once the screen door slammed behind him, I dropped back to the sofa with a groan. That last step hurt like hell.

Sliding off my sock, I surveyed the damage. The bruising had started, but the swelling really wasn't bad. I bent the foot in all directions and other than some tenderness to the touch just below the big toe, there didn't seem to be any other injuries. It definitely wasn't broken, and by the shape of the mark beneath the bruise, I was pretty certain the bulk of the hammer hit the floor.

Nice to know that awful thud was from the tool hitting aged linoleum and not my poor appendage. Hearing footsteps on the porch, I slid the sock back on and launched to my feet to pretend I'd been standing the whole time.

Calvin stopped at the living room entrance, sneakers in hand and shaking his head. "You aren't fooling anyone, you know."

Squaring my shoulders, I said, "I don't know what you're talking about."

He pointed to the large picture window behind me, which looked out over the front yard and to the street beyond. Right to where my car was parked on the curb.

Dang it.

Embracing my right to remain silent, I changed the subject as he handed over the shoes. "Do we have a start date for the work yet?"

Calvin rolled with the change. "Tentative date is next week."

I dropped onto the couch to put my shoes on. "For real? The demo can begin?" We'd already lost weeks since I'd closed on the house. The longer this took, the longer I'd have to live in a construction zone.

"Yeah, I have the crew lined up for Wednesday. The dumpster should be on site on Monday."

Once the right shoe was tied, I switched to the left, holding in the wince as I slipped my foot in. The swelling had gone down thanks to the ice, but I still loosened the laces as much as possible. Tying it wasn't going to happen, but as I stood I found the support helped a lot for walking.

"I need to get back to work." Unsure what else to say, I added, "Thanks for the frozen peas."

That would go down as one of the dumbest things I'd ever said.

He laughed. "You're welcome. I should probably get them back in the freezer."

"Right. I'll be going then."

"Are you not going to drive me back over?"

"I thought we were finished for today."

"My truck is still over there, and I have more measurements to take." Calvin grabbed the frozen vegetables and towel off the coffee table. "Are you working this weekend?"

I worked every weekend, but the wedding this Saturday was a morning affair and the bride had assured me the festivities would end around noon. Sunday was always dinner with Mom and Dad.

"Do you need me to look at something for the house? I should have time Saturday afternoon."

Calvin disappeared into the kitchen. I heard the fridge open and close, then there was a quiet pause before he returned. When he did, he extended a small sheet of paper my way. "Meet me at this address around two."

Note in hand, I read the address, which wasn't far from Bammy's house. "What are we looking at?"

"Just be there."

Why so secretive all of a sudden? "For what?"

"You'll see." He tossed me my keys. "Let's go."

Calvin strolled off toward the door, and when I rounded the corner, he was waiting with the door open.

"Are you really not going to tell me?"

"I thought you needed to get back to work."

The man was impossible. "It would help to know what I'm going to look at so I can think about what I want."

He let me pass, then closed the door behind us. "You've never not known what you want."

I took that as a compliment. "That's a good thing, right?"

Calvin remained silent and as I didn't want to have the *pick a fight* conversation again, I did the same.

"WHAT WERE YOU THINKING?" Josie asked before going back to blowing on her cup of coffee.

We were sitting in the hospital cafeteria waiting for Megan to arrive. Lindsey was upstairs with Becca, who was being induced to get little Noah into the world as soon as possible. Both baby and mother were healthy, but the baby was also nearly as big as the mother at this point. If he grew anymore, they might never get him out.

Hence, the induction.

Thankfully, Miles was handling Jacob, who was both panicked and a bit in denial. You'd never know the man had been through this once before.

"I was thinking I'd swing the hammer and the cabinet would break," I replied. "Breaking myself never crossed my mind."

To be fair, both Calvin and I were correct that the foot wasn't broken, but per a late day visit to an urgent care, I did have a deep bone bruise that would take quite some time to heal. I could only wear hard-soled shoes until then. Heels were out of the question, but I gave up wearing those for work years ago.

No matter how fancy the wedding, my job required that I not only get pics from every angle, but do so without disturbing the event. That was only possible in sensible shoes.

"That bruise looks awful. Can you really walk on it?"

"I can, but I won't be running, or even jogging, any time soon."

"There you guys are." Megan rushed up to the table. "Am I too late? Is the baby here?"

Josie shook her head and tapped the table beside her. "They just started the Pitocin less than thirty minutes ago. The doctor said it could still be hours. Have a seat."

She slowly lowered into the chair. "Shouldn't we be upstairs?"

As much as we all loved Becca, she wasn't quite herself during this ordeal. Not that we blamed her.

"Becca is a little..." Josie searched for the right word.

"Snippy," I finished for her.

Understanding in her eyes, Megan nodded. "I see. Is Lindsey with her?"

"Yep." I added sweetener to my coffee, attempting to cover the burnt taste. "She seems to be the only one who can keep Becca calm."

"What about Jacob?"

"He's getting the worst of it," Josie said. "Poor guy doesn't know whether to beg for forgiveness, or hide in the waiting room. One minute she's saying how happy she is that they're about to be parents, and the next she's cursing him for getting too close to her." Changing the subject, she said, "Ask Donna about her foot."

I failed to hide the eye roll. "Is that really necessary?"

"What did you do?" Megan asked.

"It's just a little bruise."

"Ask her *how* she bruised it."

This was the last time I was telling the story. "Calvin and I were taking some measurements at the house and he encouraged me to demo the kitchen."

Megan blinked. "I'm sorry, what?"

"Right?" Josie laughed. "I think she was trying to impress her contractor."

I may have been having improper thoughts about Calvin, but impressing him was not on my mind when I swung that hammer.

"Do you like him?" Megan asked. "You never like anyone."

"I like people." My friends stared in accusatory silence. "Okay, not a lot of people, but some. And no, I wasn't trying to impress Calvin. We've known each other since grade school. He's just an old friend."

Josie's blonde hair swooped forward and she sat up straighter. "You didn't tell us that. So you two have a history?"

You could say that.

"He grew up a couple blocks from Bammy's, so we ran with the same crowd during the summers. I hadn't seen him in years before Darnell called him over the day we first walked through the house."

"Wait, he was there the first day, but it took weeks to get him to do the job? What was his problem?"

Should I unfairly throw him under the bus, or fess up? After we'd cleared up the misunderstandings of the past, framing him as the villain felt wrong.

"Calvin wasn't the problem. I didn't want to hire him."

Megan poked my knee. "What? Why not?"

Might as well spill it all. "I didn't think he liked me much when we were kids, and when I had a crush on him early on in high school, he never gave me a second look. So I was holding a grudge."

"You do that," Megan said. I wanted to argue, but she was right.

"Anyway, once all the other contractors were a no, I gave in and offered him the project."

"What about the grudge?" Josie asked.

"Before the hammer incident, we cleared up some old misunderstandings. Let's just say, I read things wrong back then." The pair exchanged a look and I knew what would come next. "Yes, he also had a crush on me, but that was more than fifteen years ago. Ancient history. Now we're home-owner and contractor. Nothing more."

Josie turned to Megan. "Do you believe that?"

The brunette grinned. "Not for a minute."

I opened my mouth to argue when all three of our phones went off. Reading the message aloud, Josie said, *"The eagle is about to land. Get your butts up here."*

Quickly gathering our things, we hurried out of the cafeteria and I tossed my coffee on the way. No amount of sweetener would help that drink.

"We're going to have a baby," Megan trilled as we shuffled toward the elevator. "I can't believe one of us is going to be a mom."

"And the rest of us will be the best aunts any kid could hope for," Josie added.

"Spoil him rotten and give him back," I said.

Megan giggled. "This is going to be so fun."

Chapter Eight

Fun was not the word Becca would have used. For her, labor was anything *but* fun. Despite it all, she'd been a total trooper, and after ten intense hours, Baby Noah entered the world with a scream that could peel paint.

Bless his little heart. And lungs. And his perfect little toes and itty bitty fingers and the fullest head of dark hair I'd ever seen on a newborn. According to the nurses, this explained Becca's bout with heartburn in the later stages of the pregnancy.

Once the little guy was cleaned up and had spent quality bonding time on Becca's chest, we each got cuddle time of our own. When Josie, Megan, and I headed for the exit, the exhausted but elated new parents were video chatting with Jacob's parents in South Korea. His mom's tears of joy almost got to me.

The late night made getting up for the morning wedding that much harder, but I was at the church with plenty of time to spare. The day went off without a hitch, and I considered suggesting that the bride join Becca's company, because she'd planned the entire thing herself. I'd never seen an event more organized in my life, and after more than ten years of being a wedding photographer, that was saying something.

As promised, the festivities ended just after noon, at which point the bride and groom, a lovely couple in their early fifties and both on their second marriage, headed for the airport to hop a flight to Paris.

I seriously wanted to be them when I grew up.

After a stop at home to change clothes and do a quick review of the wedding shots, I sent the best ones to the bride's phone, as requested, then headed out to meet Calvin. I'd spend more time editing all of the photos into a beautiful collection at the start of the week.

Following where my GPS led, I was surprised to arrive at a non-descript garage with no sign to give away exactly why I was there. The only items I had left to choose were the appliances, but this did not look like an appliance store to me.

Far from it.

Checking the address again, I clicked back to make sure I hadn't entered a number wrong in the GPS. Nope, this was it.

There were plenty of cars in the lot, but no people. In fact, the place looked deserted. Was this a joke? Seconds before I was about to leave, Calvin's truck pulled into the lot. He pulled up close to one of the large bay doors. So close I thought he was going to drive into it, but at the last moment the door started to open.

Curious, I leaned forward to get a glimpse inside before Calvin pulled all the way in. Except he didn't. Instead, he climbed out of the truck and motioned for me to come closer. I didn't even think he knew I was there. When I opened my door and stepped out, he yelled for me to bring the car. Odd, but I did as asked.

As I put Loretta in park next to Calvin's truck, a familiar face stepped out of the garage.

"Lucas?" I said, hopping out. "Lucas Winters?"

A gleaming white smile split his handsome face. "Donna B? Is that you? Girl, where you been hiding all these years?"

I was instantly sixteen again. Lucas had been my favorite person in the neighborhood. Other than my cousins, of course. Beautiful, ridiculously smart, and just as mischievous, he'd always been ready with a smile and a laugh. Especially for Bammy. I'd probably liked him so much because Bammy had declared him one of her favorites.

When he opened his arms, I walked straight in for the hug and found my feet dangling off the ground a second later. Laughing, I said, "I've been working on becoming a self-made woman." Careful not to put too much weight on my left foot when he put me down, I leaned back. "What about you? I haven't seen you in forever."

"I'm a self-made man, darlin'. This is my shop. Repair. Restoration. A little comprehensive collision work. We do it all at Winters Body Shop."

What were we going to get from a body shop that would work in the house? Looking to Calvin for answers, I caught the annoyed look on his face. We hadn't even exchanged greetings so I wasn't sure what I could have done to earn that look.

"Come on inside," Lucas said. "I'll show you around."

He led us through the open garage and as he fell into step beside me, Calvin mumbled, "Why didn't I get a greeting like that when we met back up?"

That had to be a rhetorical question. "You know why."

He grumbled in reply and I ignored him. I didn't remember young Calvin being quite this moody.

After seeing an older model Camaro they were restoring, the custom paint room, which was fascinating, and finally arriving at Lucas's office, I was even more curious to know why we were here.

"So I hear you've got some car trouble," Lucas said once we were seated around his desk.

How did I not figure this out sooner? Jaw locked, I fought the urge to rip Calvin's head off.

"She has some issues, but nothing I can't handle."

"Cal says the engine dies at stop signs."

Cutting my gaze to the man on my left, I said, "Cal needs to mind his own business. I'll take care of my car."

Sensing the tension in the room, the mechanic said, "Is this not why you're here?"

Ears ringing, I kept my voice low. "I need to talk to Calvin alone for a minute."

Our friend looked concerned, but he was smart enough to know when to back away. "No problem. I'll be out in the shop."

As soon as the door clicked shut, I bolted from my chair. "Are you serious right now?

"Donna, I—"

"Who *asked* you to find me a mechanic?" I snapped, pacing the small office. "Did I in *any way* give you the impression I needed your help? Because I don't believe I did."

"I—"

"No. The answer is no. You had no business bringing me here and embarrassing me like this. I don't need your charity."

Calvin kept his mouth shut.

Furious, I turned on him. "Are you really not going to say anything?"

Dark brows arched as he met my eyes. "Are you going to let me talk?" Seething, I crossed my arms and remained silent. "Thank you. First, no, you did not ask for my help. Which is why I didn't tell you where we were meeting."

"If you knew I'd be upset, then why did you do it?"

"Because your car isn't safe right now, and I'd rather you be mad at me than have you hurt in an accident. Or worse."

How was I supposed to respond to that? "My car is fine."

"No, it isn't. Donna, this isn't about charity. I'm not paying to fix your car, and Lucas isn't offering to fix it for free. But he *will* cut you a deal, and he'll let you make payments if necessary." I opened my mouth to argue but he kept going. "Before you say that's charity, no, it isn't. You aren't special. He cuts all of us deals. I had to make payments when my truck needed a new engine last year."

Anger easing, I dropped back into my chair. I wasn't used to people doing me favors. It threw me off balance.

"I brought you here so you two could work something out, and you could be safe on the road. That's all. What you do from here is up to you. "

So his intentions were in the right place. He still should

have told me what this was about instead of blindsiding me in front of Lucas. There was also the issue of leaving my car here to be fixed. What was I supposed to drive?

Becca didn't have a license so she depended on the hired car apps. I supposed I could do that, but I'd rather not. Shooting weddings required hauling around delicate equipment. Doing so in hired cars would be inconvenient and potentially dangerous.

"Not that it's any of your business," I said, "but I plan to put the car in the shop as soon as I have the means for a rental." Yes, I could charge one, but I didn't like credit cards. They were for emergencies only, which this was not.

"Lucas can give you a lender." When I huffed, he added, "Again, that's a courtesy he extends to all of his clients. At least the ones he knows really well. I'm sure that includes you."

Grumbling, I said, "You should have told me."

Calvin conceded the point. "I should have. I apologize. Next time, I'll give you a heads up."

"There won't be a next time. I don't need you doing favors for me."

Looking entirely unconcerned, he leaned back in his chair. "If you're worried about owing me, forget it. I don't expect anything in return."

Of course he didn't. I should start calling him Saint Calvin. But that wasn't my issue. I just didn't like depending on people. That was the quickest and surest route to being let down. Realizing a key to his personality, I shook my head.

"You can't help yourself, can you?" I asked.

"What do you mean?"

"You're a fixer. Professionally, but also as a person. You see a problem and you can't help but find a solution, even when it isn't your problem to solve."

He didn't argue. "You make that sound like a bad thing."

"Sticking your nose into other people's business *is* a bad thing."

Lips pursed, he watched me for several seconds before replying. "There's a difference between fixing things, and presenting a solution. The person still has a choice. They can take it or leave it. Like right now. I've presented an option. You get to decide if you want to take it."

"I should have had a choice in whether or not to come here."

As patiently as ever, the saint tapped my knee with a grin. "Anyone ever tell you you might have control issues?"

I fought the smile with every bone in my body.

"Anyone ever tell you to go to—"

"Okay, Lucas," Calvin yelled. "We're good in here."

"You sure?" he said, obviously standing right outside the door.

"We're sure," I said, conceding this one to Calvin. "Come tell me how you're going to fix my car."

I NEVER IMAGINED my day would start with a flying toilet.

After rescheduling three appointments, I managed to clear my calendar for demo day. Loretta was still in the shop, so I parked the loaner—a like new Volkswagen Jetta—behind the house. No sooner did I put the car in park than a toilet shot out an upstairs window and landed with a crash in the dumpster mere feet in front of me.

Did I just see what I think I saw?

I opened my door only to have a sink drop like a rock into the dumpster and send bits of porcelain into the air. This was not the place to park a car I didn't own. Or one I did own, for that matter.

After driving around front and parking safely on the curb, I made my way into the house. The front door was open, and what could have been the sounds of demo, or someone testing small bombs, echoed off the bare walls.

The previous toilet spotting told me they'd started upstairs, but as I set foot on the first stair, Calvin spoke from behind me.

"What are you doing here?" Looking me up and down, he added, "And why are you dressed like that?"

"You said I could help with demo."

His eyes went wide. "You were serious?"

Was he not listening? "Of course, I was." Looking down at my jeans, brand new and very sturdy work boots—laced somewhat loosely on the left foot—and white tee, I asked, "What's wrong with what I'm wearing?"

Typically when we met up for house stuff, I was either going to or coming from an appointment. That meant I was in work mode, which was sleek and professional. I had to project an image that let customers know I could do the job. Weddings were considered by most as a once in a lifetime day, regardless of how often that proved to be untrue.

There were no do-overs in wedding photography. That meant couples put *a lot* of trust in me, and I never wanted them to be disappointed. A professional appearance and demeanor were absolutely critical to earning that trust.

At the same time, this didn't mean I couldn't dress down and get a little dirty.

"Well... I mean..." Calvin stammered.

Why was he acted so flustered?

"Is there a demo uniform I don't know about? Please don't tell me this requires those hideous overalls."

A strong hand rubbed his cropped hair. "No, you're good. I'm just not used to seeing you like this."

"Like what?"

"Like...normal."

This man was making no sense. "Do I get to break stuff, or not?" Before I forgot, I said, "And why did a toilet fly out of my upstairs window a minute ago?"

Calvin offered a sheepish grin. "The old ones can be kind of nasty so we don't like to bring them through the house if we can help it."

Made sense.

"Okay, then. Where do you want me?" The look that crossed his face said he was no longer thinking about demo, and it was my turn to stammer. "I mean... I... Where should I start?"

Lingering there in the foyer, both of us acting like awkward teenagers, made me think this is how it might have been back in the day if he'd had the guts to ask me out. Who knew where we'd be now if that ever happened. Probably the same place we were now.

That teenage crush would have eventually faded, and we'd have gone our separate ways. Though, why was I even thinking about this? The past was the past, and it needed to stay there.

"Hey, gang!" Calvin yelled without warning, scaring the bejeebers out of me. "Come down and meet the new member of the team."

I heard them before I saw them and backed away from the stairs, expecting a herd of buffalo to appear. One by one, familiar faces came into view, and I was starting to think that Calvin either hired or patronized every single person who grew up within a six block radius of this house.

As if I didn't know them already, Calvin made the introductions.

"This is Pretty Boy, Socks, Lenny, and Bill." He pointed to each as he said their names. "You guys know Donna. She's helping out today."

I remembered all of them.

Pretty Boy, aka Bradley Andrews, had more than grown into his nickname. He'd been handsome as a teen, but now he could easily fit in on a high fashion runway. You could cut paper on that jawline, and the amber eyes were still as striking as ever.

Socks, or Winston when his mom called him in for dinner, hadn't changed at all. Short, pear-shaped, and wearing dark-rimmed glasses that magnified his eyes to an alarming degree. I noticed his nickname still fit as well. The man still didn't wear socks.

I couldn't recall who first gave him the moniker, but he was so well known for his lack of the apparel that once someone said it, it stuck. Lenny and Bill had familiar faces, but I didn't interact with them much in the past. Neither had ever done anything to garner my attention, for good or for bad.

"Where did you go?" said a voice from the living room and I spun to see a towering figure wearing cut-off jean shorts, a Pitt T-shirt, and an Iron City ball cap coming our way. "Hey," the young woman said. "What's going on?"

"Donna's here to help," Calvin said.

"Help with demo?" she asked, looking me up and down. "For real?"

Feeling judged, I said, "Is that a problem?"

"It's a shock, is what it is."

"It's her house, JoJo. She can help if she wants to."

The name rang a bell. "*Little* JoJo? Your cousin, Little JoJo?" The last time I saw her she was maybe six years old and a tiny little thing. The grown woman before me had to be pushing six foot two at the very least. This could not be the same person.

The cold expression softened. "You remember me?"

"I remember you being a wisp of a thing. How did you get so tall?"

JoJo shrugged. "I ate my vegetables, I guess."

"JoJo got a full ride to Pitt to play basketball," Calvin said with pride. "She helps out when she has time."

Basketball. That made sense.

When she joined the others near the stairs I nearly laughed. JoJo was easily the tallest of the bunch.

"Bill and Socks, you can keep working on the bathroom. Lenny and Pretty Boy, keep pulling carpets, and move on to taking off the doors when you're finished." Calvin turned to me. "Since you got the kitchen started, you might as well help finish the job."

The guys went back upstairs, and JoJo fell into step beside me as we followed Calvin into the kitchen.

"You really remember me?" she asked, hints of the little girl apparent in her tone if not her appearance.

I nodded. "I do. You were always in a dress. Usually pink, And you hated when people called you Jolene."

Her face twisted in disgust. "I still hate that."

"It's worse when they sing it at you, isn't it?"

"You have no idea."

Chapter Nine

THE KITCHEN LOOKED VERY DIFFERENT FROM THE LAST time I saw it. The counter top was completely gone, along with the sink and faucet, the upper cabinets were nowhere in sight, and the bottom cabinets remained but without the doors. The ancient appliances had been removed, and a section of linoleum near the back door had been ripped up.

"Jo, you can go back to pulling up the floor," Calvin said, reaching for the sledgehammer that had been my nemesis less than a week ago. To me he said, "You can help me with the wall." He pulled a regular hammer off a loop on his tool belt. "Break through the drywall like this." With short, quick movements, he punched a series of small holes into the wall. "Got it?"

Not that I wasn't happy to use a more manageable tool, but I still had to give him a hard time. "So you get the big one, and I get this dinky thing?"

"This dinky thing is less likely to break your foot. Though I see you wore the right boots this time."

"I wasn't told to dress for demolition at our last meeting. That was on you."

"Yeah, it was." Calvin turned serious. "How's your foot? Are you sure you're okay to be on it like this?"

His concern made me less inclined to harass him.

"It's still tender to the touch, and has turned an ugly shade of yellow, but I can put weight on it." I wiggled the foot in question. "The boot isn't tied super tight, but tight enough to keep it on."

With a sigh, he said, "I'm really sorry."

There was no need for apologies. "We've been over this, Calvin. Neither of us had any idea I'd drop the hammer. Forget about it."

"I'm still going to watch you like a hawk today." He handed over the small hammer along with a pair of safety glasses. "You work on this side, and I'll get started over here."

Stepping to the other side of the doorway, he used the flat part at the top of the hammer to put a series of sizable holes down the drywall. His movements were efficient, steady, and caused the muscles in his arm to bulge beneath the sleeve of his dark gray tee. Instead of attacking my own wall, I got lost watching him work. Until he stopped and looked over, one brow arched high.

Heat rolled up my cheeks as I realized I'd been busted. Clearing my throat, I got to work adding to the small holes Calvin had already created. Within minutes, my hands hurt like crazy. I was used to balancing the weight of a camera, but this constant movement was proving more taxing.

Part of me wanted to take a break, but my pride wouldn't let me. When I couldn't stand it anymore, I stopped to shake out each hand. As soon as I did, Calvin handed over a pair of dark brown gloves.

"Wear these."

"I don't—" He stopped my protest with one knowing look.

Mouth shut, I put them on and went back to work. They really did make a difference, and before long, my little holes turned into one big one.

"Now do this." Calvin reached past my shoulder to rip out large sections of drywall with his hand. "Pull it all away until the beams are fully exposed, but don't go beyond that point." To my left was a spray painted white line from ceiling to floor. "That's where the opening will start."

Proud that I'd accomplished so much, I looked over to see that he'd cleared out his entire section and gone to work on the living room side of the wall. I reminded myself that this was not a competition, and, *of course*, the pro would be faster than I was. I'd be concerned if he wasn't.

None of that meant I wouldn't try to keep up.

Within an hour, we'd removed the rest of the drywall, and Calvin then used some really cool looking saw thing to cut away the beams until the doorway was twice the size it'd been when we started. Stepping back, I marveled at how much bigger the space felt already.

JoJo had worked around us until we switched over to the living room side to finish cutting the beams, but by the time the opening was done, she'd ripped up the top layer of linoleum to reveal at least two more layers beneath. I recognized the terra cotta orange flower pattern.

"I remember that from when I was little. Is that the original one?" I asked, pointing to the pattern I'd never seen before. Small white, yellow, and light orange squares of varying sizes created a pattern that screamed the seventies.

"Looks like it." Calvin tested to see if there was anything beneath that layer. "Yeah, that's it. Do you want to keep a piece of it?"

Keeping remnants of things hadn't occurred to me, but this was the design that Bammy had picked. The idea of having even a small piece suddenly felt incredibly important.

"I would, yeah. Can we do that?"

"We can do anything you want," JoJo said. Using a small metal scraper, she gently peeled up a one foot section, keeping it perfectly intact. "Here you go."

Tears welled up in my eyes, and I imagined Bammy smiling at her brand new floor. She was so proud of this house. So proud of what she and Pops had built. Now I would add to the foundation they'd established so long ago.

"Thank you."

"No problem," she said. "You could always put something like that in the new kitchen. Retro is in."

That idea dried up the tears. "I do *not* want this ugly floor in my kitchen." We all laughed. "But I might frame this piece and put it somewhere." Staring at the remnant, I said, "We could put something similar in the new powder room. These shades of yellow and orange could be pretty."

Calvin nodded. "We can do that."

We locked eyes for several seconds and I knew in that moment. He got it. He understood what this house meant to me when no one else did. The thought made me smile and I knew there was never anyone else who could have done this project with me. Calvin was the only one.

"I'll start cleaning up the drywall," JoJo said, hopping up off the floor.

Her quick departure reminded me I was here to work, not to get weepy over ancient linoleum. "What do we do next?"

"You feel up to helping pull out the rest of these cabinets?"

"Sure." We both stood and I looked around for a safe place to put my new treasure.

"Here." Calvin took the thin piece and carried it into the foyer. Returning, he said, "It'll be safe in there."

Who knew that protecting a piece of old flooring would feel like an act of wooing. The thought freaked me out. That was not what was happening here. No wooing. Absolutely not.

Determined to stay on task, I put my gloves back on, but as I looked up, Calvin reached out a hand.

"Hold on," he whispered. His breath warmed my cheek as he gently removed something from my hair. Meeting what I could only assume was my wide-eyed stare, he offered a crooked grin that curled my toes. Even my sore ones. "You had some drywall stuck there."

Unable to speak, I nodded. Maybe a little wooing wasn't so bad.

———

THE DAY AFTER THE DEMO, every muscle in my body ached. Muscles I didn't even know I had were angry. The soreness gave me a new respect for people who did that kind of work all the time. There was no way I'd have made it through my wedding shoot on Saturday without slathering on half a tube of muscle cream.

By Sunday dinner, I could at least exit a chair without moaning, though twisting too far the wrong way still elicited an uncontrollable whimper. I'd gotten through helping Mom prepare the meal without wincing, but when I reached too far for the potatoes, the truth was out.

"What did you do?" Mom asked.

"I've been helping at the house."

"Helping?" Dad repeated. "Helping with what?"

I buttered one of Mom's homemade yeast rolls. "With the demo. Before we can fix it up we have to take out the stuff that's already there. Counters, floors, some walls."

Mom stopped with a spoonful of potatoes in mid-air. "You helped knock out a wall?"

"I did." Proud of my blisters, I held out my hand. "See. These are from the hammer."

"Donna Loraine," Dad said, "you hurt yourself in that house just last week. You're paying people to do this work. Let them earn their money."

Calvin and his team more than earned their money, as far as I was concerned. My contribution was nothing compared to theirs.

"It's called sweat equity, Dad. No one made me do it. I wanted to take part in getting things started. Don't worry. I won't be helping them put it back together." I hoped to contribute to the work somehow, but he didn't need to know that. "We uncovered the original linoleum from when the house was built. Do you remember it?"

Dad loaded his plate. "I spent hours playing on that floor. Of course, I remember it. That was the ugliest floor ever."

The flowery one was, maybe, but not the original. "No it wasn't. Those little squares are kind of fun. I plan to find something similar for the new powder room we're putting in under the stairs."

"You're adding a bathroom?" Mom asked.

"I'm adding two, actually. One of the bedrooms will be split into an ensuite and a walk in closet for my bedroom. It's going to be amazing."

They set down their forks almost in unison. "Donna, have you thought this through?" Mom said.

"Thought what through?"

"This renovation. Are you sure the money you're putting into this will be worth it?"

I didn't understand the question. "What do you mean by worth it? This is going to be my forever home, so I'm making it exactly what I want."

Dad steepled his fingers in front of his nose. "You might do too much."

How could I do too much? This was my house. I wasn't putting in a swimming pool or a bowling alley. I had a budget and everything Calvin and I had planned out fit within that number.

"You guys need to stop worrying. I'm not doing anything crazy."

"Knocking out walls and adding bathrooms sounds crazy. Think about the resale value."

The resale value was going to be way higher than what I paid for it, but none of that mattered because I wouldn't be selling the house. Ever.

"Did you miss the forever house part?" I looked from one to the other and both stared back with concern in their eyes. "What are you two dancing around?"

Mom lifted her fork again. "That isn't the best neighborhood. Your property value will go up only so far. If you'd bought a house over here by us—"

"We've been over this," I said through clenched teeth. "I don't want to live over here. I want to live in Bammy's house. And Calvin is working hard to improve the neighborhood. It isn't like it used to be. He's already flipped several houses and plans to do more."

"Short of picking up the houses and moving them somewhere else, I doubt there's much anyone can do to change that area."

That's when it hit me. My parents believed they were too good for Bammy's neighborhood. They'd gotten out and had this big house in a nicer part of town so now they were, what? In a better class of people? Too good for Lofton Street? Better than the people they grew up with?

Bammy belonged in that neighborhood, and she loved living there. She was *proud* to live there. What did they think of her? That she was beneath them, too?

Putting down my fork, I lifted the napkin off my lap and set it on the table. "I've bought the house, and I'm going to live in it. Before I do that, I'm going to make it exactly what I want, while preserving the love and pride Bammy put into it." Rising to my feet, I added, "I'm not worried what the house will be worth, because I know what it's worth *to me.* Considering you grew up there, Dad, I'd think you'd feel the same. When it's finished you can visit or not visit, but you aren't going to insult my house or my neighbors."

"Sit down," Dad said. "You're being too sensitive. We're only trying to make you see the reality of the situation. It's a bad investment, honey."

How could he say that? "No, it isn't, and if you'd get your nose out of the air and go see it, you'd know that." I pushed in my chair. "I'm tired of defending this decision. Believe what you want, but remember, this is where *you* came from. Think about that before insulting everyone who's still there."

Mom leapt to her feet. "Donna, don't go. We don't have to talk about it."

I brushed her hand off my arm. "I'm not hungry anymore, and I have work to catch up on."

Before I reached the door, she said, "We'll see you next Sunday, right?"

Would they? This was the only time I ever saw them. They never came to my apartment. Never asked for a random lunch meet up. I came here every Sunday, for every holiday and celebration, but they never came to me. In fact, I could count on one hand the number of times they'd visited my apartment, and I'd lived there for six years.

"I don't know," I said honestly. "We'll see."

Chapter Ten

TINY FINGERS WRAPPED AROUND MY THUMB AND MY heart melted. "Becca, he's perfect."

The exhausted mother smiled. "He is, isn't he? Sometimes I just stare at him, wondering how I could love anyone this much."

I had to admit, holding him in my lap, staring into his big brown eyes, and marveling at the full head of dark hair did create a slight tug in the vicinity of my ovaries. But then he farted, his face twisted into a very displeased expression, and he let out a loud wail.

Ovaries came back to reality.

"I've got him," Jacob said, charging into the room and sweeping his son into his arms. He cooed as the pair disappeared around the corner, and Noah calmed before they were even out of sight.

As my friend watched her little family leave the room, I watched her. The happiness on her face was the best thing

I'd seen in days. "They're both perfect," I said. "You owe Lindsey at least a new car."

She laughed. "You forget that I technically met him by chance *before* she set us up."

"Yes, but you nearly blew it, remember? She's the one who pulled out the assist in the end."

Now Becca made an unpleasant face. "I don't like to think about things not working out."

"There's no need to," I said, waving her words away. "You two were clearly meant to be."

We fell into a comfortable silence, until she said, "Are you going to tell me what's going on?"

I shrugged. "What do you mean?"

She tilted her head. "It's Sunday afternoon. We both know where you're supposed to be. Spill."

I'd debated all week about whether to attend Sunday dinner. By Wednesday I'd decided that if they apologized for second-guessing my decision and the assumptions they made about the neighborhood, I would go. The apology never came.

Mom called on Thursday and left me a voicemail about someone at her church looking for a photographer, but there was no mention of the discussion over dinner, let alone an apology. I knew how they operated. They assumed I'd come to dinner and we'd all pretend the argument never happened. In the back of their minds, they assumed I'd come around and see the situation just like they did.

That was not going to happen.

"We had a disagreement over dinner last week."

"You and your parents?" she asked.

"Yeah." Plucking a cat hair off my pants, I sighed. "They think I made a mistake buying Bammy's house, and that I shouldn't want to live in that neighborhood. I really don't get it. That's where Dad grew up. How could he not feel the same attachment to the place that I do?"

"His childhood was probably different from yours. Wasn't your grandfather a bit unreliable when they were kids?"

"Yeah, but Pops still managed to build that house for his family. Shouldn't that make it mean even more to him?"

Her expression softened and Becca joined me on the couch. "We all live with our own ghosts, hon. Maybe his are in that house."

Maybe, but he'd never said anything to give that impression.

"I don't think that's it. They keep bringing up the property value and how much money I'm putting into the house." Curling my legs under me, I leaned my head on the back of the sofa. "You guys brought it up during breakfast that one time, too. I get that this isn't the best neighborhood in the city, but it isn't the worst either. Calvin has flipped a bunch of houses, and he's working hard to improve the area."

"He sounds like a good guy."

"He is. If Mom and Dad would come see what he's done, they'd understand and stop giving me a hard time."

Becca mimicked my pose. "Have you told them that?"

I nodded. "Yeah, I did."

"What did they say?"

"Nothing, and other than a message about someone looking for a photographer, I haven't heard from either of them since." Becca's cat Milo leapt onto the couch and curled up between us. "You know, they never come visit me. If I didn't go over there every week, I'd never see them."

"Have you invited them over?"

"I've offered to host the Sunday dinner several times, and they always give some excuse why we need to keep it at their place. Now I'm realizing that maybe this is part of buying the house. Like, if I have my own home, they'll be willing to come to me."

Becca reached over Milo to rub my knee. "I'm sorry they've made you feel that way. If it's any consolation, us girls are behind you all the way. We can't wait to see it all finished and have countless girls' nights on your couch."

Whoever said chosen family isn't the best never met my friends.

"My door will always be open, but you have to promise me one thing."

"Of course, anything."

"I get first dibs on babysitting the little bugger."

The new mother squirmed. "Oh, I... um..."

Letting her off the hook, I laughed. "I'm kidding. I mean, I fully intend to spoil him rotten every chance I get, and I will keep a special basket of toys just for him, but I also don't want to fight your mother to get my hands on him."

Relaxing, she wiped imaginary sweat from her forehead. "Oh, thank goodness. Mom has already declared that she's keeping him once I go back to work, and she's been finding excuses to come by nearly every day since we came home from the hospital."

"Will she have him when Jacob is out of school for the summer?"

"Not all the time, but we haven't figured out how to tell her that yet."

"Tell who what?" asked Josie as she, Megan, and Lindsey strolled into the apartment. Becca hadn't mentioned they were coming over.

"My mother that Jacob will keep the baby during the summer." Becca scooted over to make room for one of the girls. "We still have a couple of weeks before school is out so there's no rush to bring it up."

Josie swept up Milo and plopped down between me and Becca. "So what's up? Why aren't you at your parents' for dinner?"

How had Becca sent out an alert without me knowing?

"They aren't supportive of the house project," Becca answered for me. "Which makes no sense."

"Isn't that the house your dad grew up in?" Lindsey asked, settling onto the oversized stool.

"Yeah, it is. They think I should buy a place in a better part of town. Preferably, near them."

Megan took a seat in the new rocking chair. "I can understand them wanting you close to them."

"Dormont to Southside isn't exactly a road trip," I replied. "It's close enough. They still see the area the way it used to be, but, like I told Becca, Calvin has really worked to improve the whole block. As have other residents. They take pride in where they grew up, and where, for some of them, their families have lived for generations."

"Your dad doesn't have that same connection?" Lindsey asked.

"Apparently not."

Jacob returned from the bedroom with Noah high on his shoulder. Upon finding the room much fuller than when he'd left, he stopped and looked around. "Is this one of those girl talks?"

For years our group had operated with one unbreakable rule. If one of us says we need a girls chat, the rest stop what we're doing to participate. I hadn't been the one to order this gathering, but I was clearly the reason for it.

"The guys are waiting for you outside." Megan hopped from her chair with arms outstretched. "I'll take the baby."

Jacob laughed as he handed Noah over. "I guess I'm going out then."

Megan settled back into her seat while Jacob navigated around the coffee table to give his wife a kiss goodbye. Once the door clicked shut behind him, I made my feelings known.

"This was totally unnecessary. I skipped one Sunday dinner. That doesn't call for an official meeting."

"This isn't about you," Becca said. "We're here to discuss Megan's wedding."

"Oh." Self-centered much, Donna? I felt like a jerk. "What about the wedding?"

"Is there trouble in paradise?" Lindsey asked. "Are you calling it off?"

"No," Megan answered. "Of course not. The problem is we still don't have a location."

Considering one of us was a professional event planner,

this seemed like an odd topic to bring to the group. "What about that one out by Beaver you looked at?"

Becca shook her head. "Too far."

"There isn't a single hall or church with an open weekend this fall?" Josie asked.

Megan remained silent with her attention on the baby, while Becca shifted in her seat. "None that fit what the couple have in mind."

If someone had told me Megan would be a difficult bride, I'd never have believed them.

"What do they have in mind?" Lindsey asked.

Again, Megan stayed quiet, leaving Becca to answer.

"Small and intimate that would hold around fifty to seventy-five people. In the city," she continued, "but not a place that's hard to get to or doesn't offer parking. Oh, and not a church."

A silence fell over the room as we all exchanged glances. Everyone except Megan, who continued to coo at Noah and pretend we weren't talking about her.

"That's quite specific," Josie pointed out. "I assume you guys have looked at all the options that meet that description?"

Becca nodded. "We have. At least the ones that I know of. I'm hoping one of you might have an idea. Anyone heard of a new venue, or even a place that maybe doesn't typically hold weddings that could be persuaded?"

I ran through all the usual places in my head, but they would be the same ones Becca already knew about. Then I remembered there *was* a new venue in town. Would the couple use it was the question.

"There's a newer one you might not have heard of yet."

"Really?" Becca said.

Megan finally looked up from the baby. "Where?"

"Not far from my new place, actually. It's called Hick-amore House and it's been completely redone in the last year. The sign out front says they do weddings, but I don't know the capacity or what the inside looks like."

Josie pulled out her phone. "They must have a website." A few clicks later she spun the phone my way. "Is this it?"

There on her screen was the beautiful white house a few blocks from mine. "That's it."

"Let me see," Megan handed Noah off to Becca and squeezed herself onto the couch, practically sitting in Josie's lap. "That's so pretty. Is there a photo gallery of the inside?"

Josie explored the website and found a collection of pictures. Peeking over her shoulder, I spotted at least four perfect wedding photo locations. The layout was open but still cozy with plenty of the original architectural details intact. Soft modern colors ensured nothing looked dated. In fact, the entire design gave off a timeless feel.

Megan snatched the phone from Josie's hand and turned it to face Becca. "This is perfect. Can we go see this? Do you think they're open today? Can we call them?"

Becca tapped the screen, then made a face. "Says their office hours are Monday through Friday and tours are by appointment only. I'll forward the info to Amanda and have her call in the morning."

I pulled out my own phone. "Calvin renovated it. Let me message him and see if he can get you in."

"Do you think he'd do that?" Megan asked, spinning on Josie's lap.

"You're killing me, woman." Josie shoved her off to the side and moved to the chair Megan had exited, taking Noah with her as she went. "You gals deal with the wedding stuff while I get my baby time."

"I'm next," Lindsey declared as I typed the message into my phone.

Within seconds, Calvin replied and I read the message aloud. "I can be there in twenty if she wants to see it."

Megan bounced with excitement. "I can see it today? For real?"

I let him know it would take us a little longer than that to get there, but we'd see him in thirty. When he sent back an affirmative reply, I flashed her a smile. "For real. I told him we'll be there in half an hour."

The tiny bride-to-be thrust herself at me, wrapping her arms around my neck. "You're my hero, Donna."

Hugging her back, I said, "We don't know if this will work yet. I'm just getting you in the door."

She placed a wet kiss on my cheek. "It's going to be perfect. I know it." Scrambling off the couch, she hurried to the door and grabbed her shoes. "Let's go." When no one moved, she looked up with one sneaker in the air. "What's wrong? Why isn't anyone else getting their shoes on?"

"Becca can't go," Lindsey said. "None of us have room for the car seat, and we sent Jacob off with the guys, remember?"

Megan's face fell. "Oh, Right."

"I don't have to be there," Becca said. "Facetime me while you walk around. That'll be fine."

"Are you sure?" Linds asked.

The new mother waved off the question. "Of course. Megan is the one who needs to see it, and if this is the place she wants, then we can get on with the planning."

The rest of us rose to our feet and Josie passed the baby back to his mother.

"I'll drive," I said. The three women stopped moving. "My car is fixed," I explained. "No more stalling."

"Since when?" Josie asked.

"Since I left it with an old friend who has a garage last week. He not only fixed the problem, he rotated the tires, changed the oil, and gave her a tune up. Old Loretta is like a new woman. Err... car."

Megan hurried into her shoes. "Okay, then. Let's go see where I'm gonna to get married."

———

The pressure was suffocating. What if this place was awful? What if the reality didn't match the pictures? I didn't even know if there was parking or where the actual wedding would take place. The website only showed a few rooms inside, which were all lovely, but none of them suited either the ceremony or a reception.

What I also didn't think about until we arrived was that my friends were about to meet Calvin. Why that felt like a big deal I didn't know, nor did I want to think too deeply about it. Like I'd said before, he was my contractor and nothing more.

Though maybe we *were* becoming friends. Still. This

meeting shouldn't feel any different than introducing my friends to anyone else I knew.

Pulling into the entrance on the left side of the house, I followed the drive around to the back to a good sized parking area. Probably not big enough for too large a gathering, but better than nothing. There were other lots within a block or two plus additional street parking.

Across the parking lot from the house was a two-story structure with two large bay doors on the lower left side, a stretch of windows along the upper left, and what looked more like accommodation space on the right. The dark gray building with black accents was much more modern than the house, but maybe because they weren't attached the structure didn't look completely out of place.

Calvin's truck was parked near a rear entrance to the house. "I think we go in this way," I said, leading the group to the small back porch.

Before I could knock, the door swung open. "Hey," Calvin said. He wore his trademark overalls, and I was starting to think the man slept in those things. "Come on in."

Accepting the invitation, we each walked past him into what could only be called a *dream* kitchen. Soaring ceilings, white cabinetry, a square center island, stainless steel appliances, and the most gorgeous counter tops I'd ever seen glistened in the light pouring through the window over the sink.

"Look at the floor," Megan whispered almost reverently. The large rectangular tiles looked like marble and featured the same veining as the counter tops. "This is kitchen heaven."

"If the rest of the house looks like this," Josie said, "I might have to move in."

With a chuckle, Calvin said, "No long term rental option, sorry."

I made the introductions, explaining that Calvin was not only renovating Bammy's house, he'd also led the renovation on this place. As my friends complimented their surroundings, I realized how lucky I was to have him as my contractor.

I then went through each of my friends, explained that Megan was the one getting married, and let him know the wedding planner involved couldn't join us due to recently giving birth.

"It's nice to meet all of you, and I look forward to meeting the planner when she's available." To Megan he said, "Do you have a date for the wedding?"

Hesitantly, she said, "We're aiming for October fifth of this year. Are you booked for that day?"

Calvin checked something in his phone, then shook his head. "Not yet."

Megan practically danced with joy around the island.

"We haven't seen the rest of the place, yet," Lindsey reminded her. "Chill your pants."

Our friend composed herself, but excitement still shone in her eyes. "I'm just happy to have an option," she said.

I really hoped the rest of the house didn't disappoint. "Where do you guys hold the ceremonies?" I asked.

"That's the building out back." Calvin nodded toward the door we'd come in. "We can start out there."

Seconds later we stepped into the gray building, but the outside did nothing to prepare us for what we found inside.

The space was wide and open with gorgeous wood floors, tons of light, and even a bar in the back corner.

"As you might guess, this is where your ceremony would be. Do you know how many guests you're looking at?"

"We've whittled it down to sixty-five," Megan replied.

"We can hold a hundred so that's no problem. Weather permitting, we open the bay doors so the party can flow in and out, but the doors are also good for loading in equipment for a band or DJ. You also have the option of getting married in the courtyard, but some couples don't like to chance the weather. Especially here in Pittsburgh."

"Where's the courtyard?" Josie asked.

"Around the corner from the parking lot on the other side of the house. The space is suited for about seventy-five attendees, so it fits your count."

"If we choose to do it all inside, would the ceremony and reception be in here?"

"Yeah, we have a cocktail space upstairs where you would do drinks and appetizers while we transition this level for the reception."

They'd really thought of everything. "If the event happens out here, what's the house for?"

"Rental comes with full run of both buildings so typically the wedding party or family members stay in the house for a day or two leading up to the event. You'd also have to bring in your own caterer, and they'd have full access to the kitchen. There's a staging area in that back corner where they could serve from." He pointed to the corner down from the bar. "But most preparation would take place in the house."

"Does that mean the bride would get ready in the house

and have to walk over here for the wedding?" Lindsey asked. "What if it's raining?"

Calvin started walking. "We have an answer for that." We followed like ducklings behind him as he pointed down a narrow hall on our left. "This is the bathroom area for the guests." Still moving, he said, "And this is where the bride would get ready." Sweeping open a set of dark double doors, he led us into a beautiful bedroom with a large vanity, a king size bed, and random chairs and loveseats placed around the perimeter.

"Holy shazizzle," Lindsey mumbled. "This is huge."

"Why a bed, though?" Josie asked. "In a dressing room?"

"This can double as a wedding night suite," he answered. "Sometimes the couple doesn't leave for their honeymoon until the next day. This is an option so they don't have to go home or get a hotel when the party is over."

"Or if they want to ditch out of the party and do some celebrating on their own." Lindsey walked past the vanity and peeked around the corner. "Guys, this shower is bigger than my entire bathroom."

We all shuffled over to see for ourselves.

"That's for one person?" Megan asked.

Josie patted her on the shoulder. "It's for two, hon. You know, the happy couple. Though you could probably fit up to six if you wanted."

"At the same time?"

Heat shot up my cheeks as I caught Calvin's questioning gaze. "She's a librarian," I said, as if this conversation needed an explanation. "Can we see the rest of the house?"

"Sure. Follow me."

Chapter Eleven

THE NEXT TWENTY MINUTES WERE FILLED WITH OOHS and aahs as we encountered room after room of cozy perfection. Soft colors, gleaming hardwoods, soaring ceilings, and furnishings that offered a modern twist on classic designs. There was even a hidden door disguised as a bookshelf that led into a well-appointed library.

There were five bedrooms and four baths on the second floor, while the third floor featured a luxury main suite, complete with an intimate seating area and a gorgeous all white bathroom.

By the time we returned to the kitchen, Megan was sold.

"This is it," she said. "This is where I want to get married."

"Shouldn't you bring Ryan to see it first?" Josie asked.

"He'll agree with me. We *have* to get married here."

"You don't even know how much the place costs," Lindsey said.

Jaw tight, Megan rose to her full height of five foot nothing and said, "This is where I'm getting married."

Turning to Calvin, I cleared my throat. "Could you please put Megan Knox on your calendar for October fifth and text me a rate sheet and contact info? Amanda Crawford will call to work out the details. She'll be your contact person until Becca finishes her maternity leave."

"I can do that." Turning to Megan, he whipped a business card out of the front pocket of his overalls. "If you do want to show the groom, give me a call. He might want to see the special room."

"You have a *special room*?" I asked. What could be more special than that plush top floor bedroom?

"Yes, ma'am. We took inspiration from about a century ago." Flashing his pearly-whites, he added, "We call it the Speakeasy."

"Okay, yeah," Lindsey said. "We need to see that."

"Not today, I'm afraid. They're doing some repair work down there."

"Down there?" I repeated.

"Yeah, the Speakeasy is in the basement. Should be ready for viewings by the end of the week, though."

After a moment of silence, Josie said, "I guess this is mission accomplished. But we forgot to show Becca." Turning to Calvin, she asked, "Can we do another walk-through with her on the phone so she can see it?"

"Sure. Take all the time you need."

As they headed out of the kitchen, I stayed behind and Megan stopped at the swinging door to say, "Are you coming?"

"I'll catch up." Once the door swung shut, I said, "Thank you."

"I should be thanking you. We opened for bookings four months ago with almost no calls. It's been hard to get the word out."

Most of my work came through Becca's company, Three Rivers Events, but there were plenty of other planners in the city. "Have you sent your info out to the local event companies?"

"We have."

"Then how are you not sold out? This place is amazing."

"Thanks, but the problem isn't the house or the grounds. It's the location."

Meaning people didn't want to get married in this neighborhood. This was becoming an all too-familiar annoyance. "Do they bother to see it before making that decision?"

"Not often, no."

For some unknown reason, I said, "My parents think I made a mistake by buying Bammy's house."

"Do you think you made a mistake?" he asked.

"No."

Head tilted, he leaned on the island. "When are you going to start calling it your house?"

"What do you mean?"

"You always call it Bammy's house."

"It is Bammy's house."

"It *was* Bammy's house. Now it's your house. Living there won't bring her back, you know."

Was that why I was doing this? Some delusion that I

could move in and magically go back in time to those happier days?

"I know that, but I also know her spirit is there. Not in a she haunts the place kind of way, but in an I can *feel* her there way. Does that sound crazy?"

"Nah, that's true in a lot of the houses I flip. More so for you, since that's your grandmother, but there are plenty of old spirits lingering around these blocks."

"Do you think I made a mistake?" I asked. "Be honest. You know how much money this is costing me."

Calvin paused and my heart stopped. If he said the words I didn't want to hear, I might fall apart right there on his beautiful marble floor.

"If you were flipping the house with the goal of selling it right away, I'd say yeah, that's a mistake. You wouldn't get anywhere near the money back that you're putting in. But you aren't doing that. You're making yourself a home you plan to live in for a long time, right?"

"Yeah."

"Then how could that be a mistake? Sometimes spending the money is worth what you get in the end."

I liked that answer. "I don't suppose you could explain that to my parents?"

He rubbed a calloused hand over the smooth counter top. "I don't know. Meeting the parents is a big step."

If he wanted to tease, I could tease right back. "You always were afraid of Daddy."

Calvin leaned his elbows on the counter. "Your daddy is six foot four and mean."

"What? Daddy isn't mean."

"He sure was. When I came over to ask you to the spring formal that one time, he chased me off the porch."

My jaw dropped. "You're lying. You never asked me to the formal."

He straightened with a hand over his heart. "I swear on my best set of boots, I tried. He said no thug from the hood was good enough for his daughter."

The more time I spent with this man, the more my entire life became a lie.

"He never told me."

"Really? You went cold after that so I figured you knew and agreed with him."

Teenage me had been such an idiot. Eyes down, I murmured, "No, I didn't agree."

I looked up to see him watching me, but before either of us could speak, my friends plowed into the room.

"Becca, you have to see this kitchen," Josie said, holding her phone up in the air and swinging around to show the whole space. "Look at these counter tops. They're to die for."

"And the floor," Megan added. "Show her the floor."

"You're making me dizzy," Becca said. "Who is that with Donna?"

Josie pointed the phone at Calvin. "That's her hunky contractor and the genius behind this house." Tapping the screen, she shuffled around the island to stand next to our tour guide. "Becca, meet Calvin."

"Nice to meet you," she said. "I'm sorry I couldn't be there in person."

"No worries," he said, rolling with my insane friends. "I'll be happy to show you around when you're ready."

Josie whipped the phone away and said, "We're headed back. Megan has taken a ton of pics, and we have a business card for Amanda. She can thank us later for giving her the best kept secret in Pittsburgh. See ya soon and give the baby kisses for us."

"Will do."

With another tap Josie broke the connection. "Calvin, you really are our hero. This house is gorgeous, and it's going to be perfect for the wedding. I still can't believe it's available."

"Must have been meant to be," he said with a smile. "Glad I could help."

"Now I'm even more excited to see what Donna's house is going to look like." Lindsey glanced around the kitchen. "If this is the kind of work you do, her place is going to be amazing."

"In Donna's case, I'm just executing her ideas. She'll deserve the credit for how it turns out."

"A man willing to share the credit?" Josie shot me a look. "Woman, snap him up."

My mind went blank, but Calvin saved me from having to reply.

"She's too good for me. I'm just the hired help."

"We need to go," I said, far too frazzled to keep this up. "Thanks again for taking the time to show us around. We'll make sure Amanda calls soon to lock in the rental."

"No worries." Calvin opened the back door and let us exit first. "Donna, I'll call you about that thing we were discussing."

If I had my way, we wouldn't be continuing that discussion any time soon. Without looking back, I waved goodbye and hopped in the car. The girls chatted all the way back, allowing me to listen in silence. I'd essentially just admitted that I liked him back when we were kids. Something I probably should have done when he came clean that day at the house, but what did it matter?

That was a long time ago. We were adults with our own lives now. Teenage crushes had no bearing on the present. Right? Then why did I feel fifteen again and wishing I could melt into this car seat and disappear forever?

"Donna," Josie said, "how are you resisting that man? He's beautiful and an absolute sweetheart in addition to clearly being incredibly capable of just about anything. That house is more amazing than anything in my parents' neighborhood."

Her parents' neighborhood was one of the wealthiest in the city, with stately old homes that most could only dream of. "I wouldn't go that far," I said.

"I would. If I ever get married I doubt that Mom will let me get away with a guest list under a hundred, but if she did, I'd use that place in a heartbeat."

"I just want to use the shower," Lindsey tossed in.

"Ryan and I are still looking at fixer-uppers," Megan said. "If we get one, is it okay if I hire Calvin to do the work?"

It took a few seconds to realize she was talking to me. "You don't need my permission."

Lindsey leaned up from the backseat. "You never answered Josie's question."

"What question?"

"The one about how you're resisting your contractor," she

said. "Or are you? That looked pretty intense when we walked into the kitchen."

"Wait, what?" Josie said. "What did I miss?"

"I didn't notice either," Megan said.

The eagle-eyed school teacher caught my gaze in the rearview mirror. "You like him, don't you?"

I could lie, but they'd see right through me. "Yes."

Megan too leaned forward and squeezed her face up next to Lindsey's. "For real? Oh my gosh. You two would be perfect together."

"You don't even know him," I reminded her. "He could be a jerk."

"But he isn't," Josie said. "He just stopped what he was doing on a Sunday afternoon to show your friends around that big house. All because you sent him one text. That's a good guy."

I couldn't argue. "Yeah, he's a really good guy."

"Are you going to make a move?" Lindsey asked.

"I haven't decided," I answered truthfully. "We have a lot of history."

"Have you guys dated?" Megan asked.

Shaking my head, I checked the side mirror and changed lanes. "No, not yet."

Lindsey sat back with a smug smile. "That *yet* just gave you your answer."

Chapter Twelve

I barely had another free moment for the next month.

Literally.

The end of May and most of June brought the craziest wedding schedule of the year, and this season had been busier than ever. The rare moments when I wasn't working a wedding or shooting engagement photos, I was editing the previous shoot, meeting new clients, or passed out on my couch.

After multiple calls and messages from both Mom and Dad, I returned to Sunday dinners, but our conversations were strained, and we all went out of our way to avoid the subject of Bammy's house. Not that I'd had much time to think about it myself.

On the last Monday in June, I finally found the time to tackle painting my bedroom. Though Calvin sent me regular updates during the month, I was still dying to see the place in person. When I pulled up out front, I couldn't believe the difference.

Is this the same house?

The awnings were gone, as were the ugly shrubs and chain link fence. The front yard was still small but looked twice the size it had before. The ratty old screen door was gone, and the inside door stood open. As I approached the porch, I could hear random power tools, and a smell I didn't recognize assaulted my nostrils.

Stepping into the foyer, I paused to let my eyes adjust to the dimness. I also tried to figure out where the sounds were coming from. I'd promised to stay out of the way, and if I caused an issue my first day in the middle of the chaos, Calvin was going to be even more put out about me moving in early.

Once I could see again, I noticed the entrance to the new half bath where a wall had been before. Stepping closer, the potent scent got stronger. Pipes poked out of the wall on the right where I knew the small sink would go, but the toilet had already been installed. Brown paper covered the floor, I assumed to protect the tile I'd picked from a picture on my phone. This was my chance to see it in person.

Bending down, I tugged at a piece of tape to lift the paper.

"What are you doing?" boomed a voice behind me. Startled, I fell forward and cracked my head on the toilet. Calvin rushed to pick me up. "Are you okay?"

"Do you enjoy scaring people like that?" Rubbing my head, I ignored the rush of happiness that shot through my brain at the sight of him. What the heck was that about?

"I didn't scare you on purpose," he defended. "Were you ripping up that paper?"

I checked my hand for blood and thankfully found none. "I want to see the tiles."

"You know what they look like. You picked them."

"But I haven't seen them in person."

As if I weighed no more than a leaf, Calvin picked me up and placed me on my bottom just outside the bathroom door. Then he squatted and worked the tape free. A second later, still reeling from how easily he'd moved me, I got my first glimpse of the pretty tile and let out an involuntary squeal.

"Oh my gosh, it's perfect. It's almost exactly like the original tile from the kitchen."

I would never put such a busy pattern in my kitchen, but the small orange and yellow squares provided the perfect funky but cute vibe for this powder room.

"Good thing you like them because replacing them is not in the budget or the schedule."

Speaking of... "Are we still on target for both of those?"

Nearly everyone I talked to about this project felt the need to tell me that renovations always run long and go well over budget. I couldn't afford either of those scenarios.

"So far so good." Calvin stood and extended a hand to help me up. I ignored the urge to get myself up and accepted the assistance. When he leaned close and checked my forehead, I forgot to breathe. "You're going to have a bump, but it doesn't look too bad. I had no idea you were so accident prone."

Wait, what? "I'm not accident prone."

"You could have fooled me. Ready to see the other

bathroom?"

The change of topic threw me off. We hadn't finished the accident prone thing yet. *He* was the reason I kept having these accidents, not some natural inclination on my part.

"The other bathroom?" I asked, as if I had no idea what rooms were in this house.

"The hall bath upstairs. We finished it last week."

With a poke in his chest, I said, "Why didn't you tell me?"

Calvin squared his broad shoulders. "I knew you'd be here today and if I told you about it on Friday, you'd have been in here over the weekend."

Like that would be a bad thing. "It's my house. I can come in whenever I want."

"But I wasn't here over the weekend."

"And...?"

"And I want to see your face when you see it."

This man kept surprising me in the best and worst ways. It was crap like this that made me like him. While not seeing him for a month, I could tell myself that what had begun to feel like a crush was really nothing.

I was grateful that he was helping me fix the house, impressed by how patient and capable he'd proven to be, and maybe a little attracted. But who wouldn't be?

He was gorgeous, grounded, and even sensible at times. None of that meant I wanted him to be anything more than my contractor. Then he had to go and get all cute and honest and reveal how much he understood what this house meant to me and blow all of my reasoning right out of the water.

Damn him.

"Does it look good?" I asked.

Playing coy, he said, "Go see for yourself."

Like a child on Christmas morning, I took off up the stairs, the thud from Calvin's boots echoing behind me as he followed. When we reached the landing, warm hands slid over my eyes.

Leaning close to my ear, he said, "You ready?"

My whole body shivered and my mouth went dry as his scent surrounded me. Who knew musky sawdust was my thing? "I'm ready."

As if we were dancing, he shifted forward and my body went into motion. He navigated me down the hall before stopping at what I assumed was the door to the bath.

"Here it is," he said, lifting his hands away.

I blinked a few times, focusing on the scene before me. The sage green tiles, wood finish vanity, and muted brass fixtures shone in the light coming in through the small window. The stunning wall sconces added a soft glow as well.

"Oh, Calvin, it's beautiful."

"Yeah, it is. You did a great job designing it."

Nonsense. "I pointed to a few pretty things in a picture, but you brought it all to life."

Most of the pieces in the showroom image had been out of my budget, but he'd worked with Tina to get as close to the look as possible with more affordable choices. He'd even added an area rug and linens.

In that moment, my cynical, tough exterior fell away and tears filled my eyes. Instead of teasing me, as he had every right to do, Calvin rubbed my shoulders and let me cry.

After a while, he said, "I think Bammy would like it."

More tears came.

"I feel like an idiot," I said, patting my wet cheeks on my sleeves. "It's just a bathroom."

"But it's *your* bathroom," he said. "That makes a difference."

Pride swelled as the tears ebbed. "Do you really think she'd like it?"

"This makes me think so."

Suddenly a picture showed up in front of my face. There were Bammy and Pops on their old flower-pattern couch in the center of the living room. My eyes went from the picture to the bathroom and back.

"The walls are the same green."

"Yep."

How could he have a picture I'd never seen before? Snagging the photo, I spun to face him. "Where did you get this?"

Calvin took my hand and led me farther down the hall. "We found a box of pictures in the attic. I put them in your room to keep them safe."

We entered what would be my bedroom and I was once again surprised. The whole space was set up for painting. The ladder, a small table filled with rollers, brushes, and paint cans, plus large drop cloths were spread out along the base of every wall. He'd taken care of everything.

Also on the table was a stained and nearly crushed brown box. Heart suddenly on the outside of my body, I approached the new found treasure. "All of these were in the attic?"

"Yeah. Pretty Boy found them while he was checking out the wiring up there."

I picked a handful off the top and gently flipped through them. Not a single one looked familiar. "How long do you think they've been up there?"

Calvin lifted one from the box. "I haven't gone through them, but all the ones I've seen look like they're from the seventies. Definitely before either of us were born."

"Is this my dad?" I asked, pointing to a small boy sitting in the kitchen sink. The child couldn't be more than two, if that.

He leaned close until our cheeks nearly touched. "Could be. Isn't your Uncle Sonny the youngest? Could be him, too."

"You might be right." Sifting through photo after photo was like stepping back in time. Bammy and Pops on the porch swing. Dad, his brother Sonny, and his sister Jackie posing in front of the house in their Sunday best. Sonny had been gone for a few years now, after losing a battle with throat cancer.

Handing one over, Calvin said, "Isn't this your parents?"

The image showed Mom and Dad dressed in formal wear. Dad's suit was baby blue, while Mom's white dress had short, puffy sleeves and hugged her slender frame to perfection.

"Oh, wow. That might be a prom picture." Looking closer, I saw so much of myself in Mom's face. "They look really happy."

"I didn't know they were high school sweethearts."

"Yeah." I rubbed a finger over the two most important people in my life. "They didn't go to the same school, but Dad says he met her at a football game and it was love at first sight." Eyes on the image, I asked, "Do you think that's real?"

"What's real?"

"Love at first sight."

Calvin paused long enough that I looked over to see if he'd tuned me out. Eyes on mine, he said, "Yeah, it's real."

Flustered, I dropped the photographs back into the box. "I should get started on the painting, and I'm sure you need to get back to whatever it is you were doing before I got here." Stepping away, I grabbed a roll of blue tape off the table and starting covering the trim.

Why wasn't he leaving?

Half grin in place, he watched me squirm. "You sure you're good? I could help."

"No," I said far too quickly. "I'm good. I've got this. Don't let me hold you up." I shooed him away. "You can leave."

The man knew he'd made me uncomfortable and looked quite pleased with himself.

"If you need me, I'll be working out back." He pointed to the far window. "Just holler."

I would not be hollering. "It's just painting." He had the nerve to look skeptical. "I painted my entire apartment, thank you very much. I think I can handle one bedroom."

He held up his hands. "I never said you couldn't."

"Then why do you have that smug look on your face?"

Sobering, he fought to hide the smile. "What smug look? This is just my face."

And a dang pretty face it was. "You're keeping me from getting started."

"I'm leaving." He backed toward the door. "Oh, one more thing."

With a huff, I crossed my arms. "What?"

"The water is off so if you need to use the bathroom, let me know."

Because what woman didn't want to yell out a window that she had to pee?

"I'll hold it."

Calvin chuckled on his way out of the room. "Suit yourself."

———

JUST OVER AN HOUR and one full listen to the Lemonade album later, I really had to pee. Every wall was edged in, and two walls had a full first coat. But I'd made the mistake of finishing my pop, not thinking about where all that liquid was going to go.

Refusing to announce my needs to the whole neighborhood, I trudged downstairs to find Calvin and have him turn the water on. What I did not expect was to step into the kitchen and find the back wall of the house gone.

Catching myself before literally stepping off the kitchen into a pit of mud and rocks, I spotted Calvin. He stood with his back to me, hard hat covering his dark, cropped hair, speaking to three men I didn't recognize. Not wanting to interrupt, I waited until the conversation ended and he turned around.

The moment he spotted me, that irritating grin slid right back into place. Crossing the distance between us, he hopped the three feet into the kitchen as if he could fly and my ovaries did matching back flips.

"How's it going?" he asked.

"Good, but I need to go."

"You're leaving?"

He was going to make me say it.

Looking around, I leaned in and lowered my voice. "I have to pee."

"Oh," he said. As if we were cohorts in some elaborate conspiracy, he also lowered his voice. "Follow me."

As easily as he hopped up, Calvin hopped back out of the kitchen and turned my way. "Come on."

I didn't move. "Why do I need to go with you to turn on the water?"

He shook his head. "I can't turn on the water."

If he thought I was squatting in the yard he had another think coming. "Then where are we going?"

"To the porta-john."

I was not the prissy type. I didn't scream at the sight of a bug, or turn my nose up at getting a little dirty. But every woman had a line she would not cross, and for me, that was using a porta-john. Unless there was no other option for a hundred miles and the alternative was peeing on myself, this was a hard no.

"Never mind," I said, turning back into the house.

Calvin caught up in seconds. "Come on, Donna. You can't hold it forever."

"I don't plan on it. I'm going up to get my keys so I can go find a civilized bathroom."

The sound of keys jingled behind me. "Take these."

I spun around. "Why would I take your truck when I have my car?"

"Cute," he said. "I'm not offering my truck. I'm offering

my house. Walk over the two blocks and use the bathroom there."

Uncertain, I stared at the keys. "You want me to go to your house? Alone?"

"Do you need a chaperone to use the bathroom?"

Snagging the keys, I stomped past him. "I'll be back."

"That feels like a warning." As I hit the last step he yelled, "Don't talk to strangers!"

I liked him better when he wasn't trying to be funny all the time. Thankfully, he couldn't see me laugh with my back to him.

The day was warm, but not the oppressive heat we'd have in a month. I enjoyed the sun on my cheeks, the sound of children playing in the yards I passed, and the scents of honeysuckle and apple pie. Either a neighbor had one sitting near an open window, or my nose was having a flashback to when I was a kid and the scent of baked goods seemed to fill the whole block.

This felt good. Felt... right. Like I was always meant to live here, and now I would.

I reached Calvin's place within a few minutes, let myself in, and did my business. The temptation to snoop around was strong, but I feared I'd either find something disappointing, or worse, a reason to like him even more. Plus, I wouldn't want anyone sticking their nose into my business, so I'd never do such to someone else.

Locking the door on my way out, I spun and nearly plowed over a woman who'd appeared out of nowhere. Her hair was slicked back into a high ponytail, she wore a full face of makeup that appeared unfazed by the heat of the day, and the tight tee and short shorts revealed curves you could only be blessed with genetically.

"Who are you?" the stranger said.

Catching my balance, I said, "I'm Donna Bradford. Who are you?"

"What were you doing in Calvin's house?"

Her tone hit me the wrong way. "Can I help you with something?" She wasn't the only one who could answer a question with a question.

"You can't help me with anything."

The attitude was unnecessary. I'd done nothing to her, and I certainly hadn't been breaking and entering into Calvin's house. I'd have explained as much if she hadn't come at me like she owned the place.

"Then there's no need to continue this conversation. Have a nice day." I waited for her to leave, but she stood her ground and our confrontation turned into a silent stare off.

Lucky for her, I had all day.

"Are you leaving?" she finally said.

"I'll be right behind you."

She crossed her arms. "I'm not going anywhere."

Then we had a problem. "Calvin isn't here," I said. "You'll have to come back another time."

Jealousy reared its ugly head and I fought the urge to tell her not to come back at all. Calvin was my contractor. That was it. I held no claim over him, and we'd never discussed his relationship status. My assumption that he was single was on me. Maybe I'd been wrong.

The little powerhouse held up her hand, shaking a set of keys in the air. "I'll let myself in."

For a moment, I debated what to do. Did she really have a key to his house? Would he want her here when he wasn't home? Was this even any of my business?

The answer to the last was obvious.

Keeping my voice pleasant, I offered a bright smile. "You do that."

Without looking back, I carried my Lycra-covered butt off the porch and walked the two blocks back to the house. Thankfully, I didn't see Calvin on my way up to the bedroom, where I reminded myself I had no right to be angry.

The man had done nothing wrong. He never flirted or even hit on me. He'd never asked if I was single, nor did he claim to be himself. My childish crush in no way obligated him to feel the same. Besides, this is what I'd been telling myself for weeks. When this project was over, we'd go our separate ways.

Based solely on the burning in my gut and how I was struggling to unclench my jaw, my feelings had obviously changed more than I realized. Better to find out now that he was taken than make a move during a weak moment and embarrass us both.

Starting the Lemonade album over, I turned up the volume on my phone and sang along as I painted, putting a little more oomph behind some of the lyrics. A combination of anger and jealousy shifted the job into overdrive. Before long, all but one of the walls had two coats. I was on the second coat of the last wall when Calvin appeared at the bedroom door.

Time to test my acting skills.

Chapter Thirteen

"You work fast," he said, checking out the walls. "The blue-gray was a good choice."

"It's dusty blue," I corrected. Reminding myself to act cool, I finished the corner where I was working and slid the roller into the paint tray. "I like it."

"I take it you got to the house and back okay?"

"Yeah. I left your keys on the table in the foyer."

"I found them." Calvin leaned against the door frame. "We got the foundation for the addition started."

Cleaning up my mess, I nodded. "That's good." We had yet to make eye contact, and I was hoping he'd take the hint and leave me alone.

Of course, he didn't.

"I heard you ran into someone today."

His love life is none of my business.

"She was on her way in when I was leaving." Our eyes met for a split second before I said, "I'm about done in here. Do you think it'll need another coat?"

He surveyed my work. "Looks good to me, but I can check in the morning when the sun is coming straight in and let you know."

"I appreciate that." Lifting the pan with the paint and roller, I asked, "How do I wash this out since there's no water?"

Calvin crossed to the table. "Don't worry about it. Are you busy for dinner?"

Was he serious? I accidently meet his girlfriend and now he wants to take me to dinner? "I don't think that's a good idea."

"Why not?"

He was going to make me say it. "Because you shouldn't be having dinner with me when your girlfriend is at home."

"That's what I thought." He shook his head. "Jasmine isn't my girlfriend."

"Jasmine?" I repeated. "That's her name?"

"Yeah. Jasmine Riley. She moved to the block about three years ago. Her two-year-old twins have a lot of health issues so she can't hold down a regular job outside the house. She does telemarketing from home, but a few of us in the neighborhood pay her to clean to make extra money."

As much as I was dying to know all this, he owed me no explanations. He and I had a professional relationship, regardless of how much I'd pouted in my head all afternoon.

"You really don't have to explain." I bent to roll a drop cloth because I still couldn't look him in the eye. My feelings were all over the place and the last thing I needed was for him to see exactly how much thinking he had a girlfriend had affected me.

"Clearly, I do." He moved closer and said, "Donna, look at me."

Eyes closed, I exhaled, telling myself that nothing had changed from this morning. Finally, I turned his way. "What?"

"I'd like to take you to dinner."

"You don't need to reward me for painting my own bedroom."

"I'm not rewarding you." His eyes stayed locked on mine. "Will you go to dinner with me?"

I could still see the expression on Jasmine's face. That was the look of a woman who saw another sniffing around her territory.

"Does Jasmine know she isn't your girlfriend?"

"Yes."

"That's not the impression I got."

Taking a deep breath, he ran both hands over his hair, then dropped them to his sides. "She's made it clear that if I asked, she'd say yes. And I've let her know, I'm not asking."

Did I believe that? She wouldn't be the first woman to stake a claim where her flag wasn't welcome, but I also wouldn't be the first woman to fall for a lie and get herself hurt. Our history may have been filled with misunderstandings, but one thing Calvin had never been was a liar.

Relenting, I asked, "Are you buying?"

"That's the plan," he said, relaxing. "Or we can split it. Up to you."

If we split the check, then I could tell myself this was just two friends having dinner. Which is what I should have done.

"All right, you can buy."

"Then let's go."

"Now?" I looked down at my paint-covered clothes. "I'm not dressed to go out."

He looked me over with a straight face. "You look fine."

Had he been the one sniffing paint all afternoon? "I look like I've been painting all day and fell into the bucket."

"Where we're going that won't matter."

So he knew where he was taking me before he even asked. That was a big assumption.

"What if I'd said no?"

"No to what?"

"To going to dinner."

Calvin offered one of his nonchalant shrugs, and I was starting to believe nothing bothered this man.

"I'd still go, but it'll be better with you there."

One of the most lackluster yet nicest compliments I'd ever received. How could I say no after that?

"Are you sure I won't be embarrassed to go in looking like this?"

Showing a bit of impatience, he said, "I've taken the whole crew in looking way worse than that."

I chose to see that as another compliment and decided to stop pushing my luck. "Then by all means. Let's go eat."

"How DID I not know about this place?"

I lived only minutes away. How had I missed it?

Breathing deep, my mouth watered. If this wasn't what heaven smelled like, I didn't want to go.

"They've been open less than a year." Calvin waved to someone behind the counter and unleashed a flurry of sound and excitement I did not see coming. A beautiful woman in a bright red apron charged toward us, arms outstretched and an infectious smile on her lips.

"Calvin, mi querido, you know I love to see your sweet, sweet face." Cupping said face, she kissed him on both cheeks. "You always bring your friends." Stepping back, she scanned me up and down before offering an approving grin. "Ah, muy bonito. It's about time you got yourself a woman."

Calvin blushed, which was adorable as hell, and I couldn't help but tease him. "I'm not his woman. This is only our first date."

"He must really like you to bring you to Rosalie's Bodega." Tapping her chest, she beamed with pride. "Best food in town is right here. You will bring all your friends, too. Si?"

"If it tastes as good as it smells, I'll bring everyone I know." I could already see the girls devouring this place. "Do you make Huevo Rancheros?"

Pudgy hands covered her mouth as she leaned back dramatically. "Ay, carina, I make the best Huevo Rancheros you will ever have *in your life*. You want to try? I make them for you right now."

I didn't want to put her out. "I'm sure those aren't on your dinner menu. Don't go out of your way for me."

"Disparates. I make them now." Shooing us toward the tables, Rosalie said, "Sit down and I'll send Rodrigo. He'll take good care of you."

We did as told, crossing the blue and yellow checkered floor to take our seats at one of the high tables.

Settling onto a tall stool, I took in my surroundings. "This has to be the most colorful restaurant in town." Primary colors covered every surface, from the yellow poles down the center of the space to the bright blue table legs. "I take it you're a regular here?"

Calvin nodded. "Rosalie moved to the neighborhood about ten years ago. She started with a food truck, and was able to upgrade to this site late last year."

The fact we were her only patrons concerned me. "How's it going for her?"

He rubbed his hands together, tilting his head from side to side like he was trying to crack his neck. "Things started slow, like most places do, but it's picking up."

A man I assumed to be Rodrigo arrived with a basket of chips and salsa, which I could immediately tell were homemade. Not that I expected any less. What I didn't expect was for Calvin to have a full conversation with the waiter *in Spanish.*

I caught enough to know that Calvin ordered himself tacos and confirmed my order of Huevo Rancheros. There were drinks in there somewhere, but the only word that sounded familiar was the one I thought meant water.

When Rodrigo walked away to pass on whatever he'd written on his little notepad, I stared at my date with raised brows.

Catching the silent question, he gave a nonchalant shrug. "I help a lot of small business owners. It made sense to learn the language."

The man was full of surprises. "How long did it take to get fluent like that?"

"About seven years." He scooped salsa onto a chip. "I ordered us Aguas Frescas. Rodrigo said they're trying a new mango flavor. I hope that's okay."

So not water after all. "That's fine." I dug into the nachos. "What do you mean you help small business owners? Help them how?"

"I walk them through the process, depending on the type of business. Everything from the license to operate to opening a bank account."

I'd done all of that, of course, many years ago. I could have used a little guidance as I was fresh out of college and had no idea what I was doing. Taking pictures was the easy part. Getting established was more complicated, even without a brick and mortar store to worry about.

"So you run the renovation business, and Hickamore House, *and* you help other business owners while learning Spanish. Is there a cape hiding under those overalls?"

He laughed. A sound I liked very much.

"I'm no hero. Just a guy who likes to help out. But since you're keeping track, I've also picked up a bit of Polish and German along the way."

Of course, he did.

"When do you sleep?" I asked, scooping up another chip. These were easily the best I'd ever had. "I feel bad taking up your time. Don't you have three other places to be right now?"

Eyes meeting mine, he said, "I'm right where I need to be."

Very smooth. And based on my spiking temperature, I was not immune. Time to change the subject.

"How did Hickamore House come about? Was the plan always to turn it into an event venue?"

Thankfully, he rolled with the change.

"JoJo gets credit for that. Doing a simple flip wasn't feasible with a house that size. We could have broken it up into apartments, but that would have cost us a lot of the original architectural elements. No way was a single family going to buy a house that size in our neighborhood, so we were about to pass on it. Then she suggested the wedding angle, and once we worked through the numbers and how to use that old carriage house in the back, it was a no-brainer."

Not a no-brainer at all. Starting any business came with risks. They must have sunk a solid six figures into that renovation with no guarantee they'd make any of it back. After seeing the property, I recognized the potential to more than earn out, but there was still the challenge of location. Improving the neighborhood was one thing. Changing people's perceptions of the neighborhood was another.

"I feel like you're making it sound simpler than it was. That's a huge project."

Rodrigo arrived with our drinks, which were bright and orange and sporting cute little paper umbrellas. He also added small cups of queso and guacamole to the table.

"Rosalie says you must try these."

Who was I to argue with Rosalie? "Happy to."

The waiter walked away and instead of picking up where we left off, Calvin asked, "How are your parents? Have they come around on the house yet?"

He'd rolled with my topic change so it was only fair that I roll with his. "They're fine, and not really. They think I should have bought a house over in Dormont by them."

"Didn't your dad grow up in the house?"

Did I want to reveal how my parents truly felt? Not only was it embarrassing that they were so short-sighted, but the truth was also insulting to the people who still lived there. People like Calvin.

Without elaborating, I gave a partial truth. "I think they'll change their minds once they see what we do to it."

"That reminds me," he said, dunking a chip into the guac. "Not that I brought you here to talk shop, but I have a suggestion I want to run by you."

"What is it?"

"What do you think about putting French doors on your studio?"

I tried to picture it. "Like as the entrance to the room?"

"Yeah." He grabbed a napkin and whipped a pen out of his front pocket. "Clients will come up the stairs here," he said, drawing a narrow rectangle on the rough paper. "Then make a left and step through the French doors into the studio. The space will feel bigger, you'll get extra light from the window at the end of the hall, and if you need to bring in any props, you'll have an expanded doorway to get them through."

We didn't even know yet if I could have a studio, but I liked the way he was thinking. The benefit of using my loft was the soaring ceilings and wide open space for a variety of backdrops and setups. Though we were putting nine foot ceilings in the addition, I'd still be restricted in what I could do.

With a double-sized entrance, maybe not *as* restricted.

"I like the idea. Do they fit with the current plans?"

Calvin wadded up the napkin. "I'll have Sheilah make the change to the drawings based on the doors I've priced out."

Getting a little ahead of himself, wasn't he? "You already priced them out?"

"I wouldn't bring the idea to you if I didn't know it was possible. I've looked at four sets you can choose from that would all work and come in at the right price."

That made sense. I'd be more annoyed if I got excited about the idea only to learn I couldn't afford it. Picturing the possibilities, this really would make my life easier.

"Do you have any other ideas that I haven't thought of yet?" Better to get everything in now than go back and make changes later. Once this construction was finished I doubted I'd ever want to do more. Even for small projects.

Before he could answer, Rosalie and Rodrigo delivered our food. When she set my plate on the table, I could only stare at the sight before me. Two perfectly cooked, sunny-side up eggs glistened on a bed of refried beans, all floating on perfectly toasted tortillas. Salsa and queso fresco added brightness, and the food smelled so good I nearly kissed her cheeks the same way she'd kissed Calvin's.

"I have to get a picture of this."

Not that I wouldn't be seeing the dish in my dreams, but the girls needed to know what I'd discovered. Two clicks later, I put my phone away and lifted my fork. When I sliced the egg, bright yellow yoke flowed across the beans and I scooped up every ingredient into one bite.

Taking my first taste, I nearly moaned. They were better than I'd imagined. Turning to Rosalie with my mouth full of spicy goodness, I said, "Will you adopt me?"

She laughed and patted my cheek. "I have five at home. What is one more?"

To an only child, one more sounded like six too many.

"Thank you for making these. I can confirm they are the best I've ever had *in my life*." Shoveling in another bite, I gave up and released a moan of delight. How was half the city not filling this place on the daily?

As if some higher power decided to answer my question, the doors swung open and one group after another filled the tables. Rosalie went off to greet her new arrivals.

"I take it they're good?" Calvin said.

I was having such a life-changing experience I almost forgot he was there. "I can never repay you for bringing me here. If you ever need a kidney, I'm your girl."

He took a bite of his taco, set it back in its red basket, then wiped his mouth. "You'd have found the place eventually."

Did the man ever take credit for anything?

"Where did all of these people come from?" Nearly every table was full and diners were still coming in.

Calvin looked at his watch. "From work, probably. Rosalie's is a regular spot for the locals."

Lucky them. "The girls are going to love this place."

"You'll bring them here?" he asked, taco hovering halfway to his mouth.

"Heck, yeah. We have this weird thing for Mexican food.

Anytime one of us finds a new place, we all have to check it out."

"Huh," he muttered before taking a bite.

I was going to need him to elaborate. "Huh, what?"

Crunching through the taco shell, he caught a falling piece of tomato before setting the whole thing back in the basket. Holding a napkin in front of his mouth he said, "They seem more like wine and cheese on the veranda types."

"What's wrong with wine and cheese?" This was our second favorite girls' night fare.

"I didn't say there's anything wrong with it. Just that it isn't tacos out of a basket, you know?"

He'd met three of them for less than an hour, and had yet to be in the same room with Becca. Implying they were too uppity for Rosalie's Bodega ticked me off.

"You don't know anything about my friends, so don't make assumptions about them."

Calvin went for another chip. "There's no need to get mad."

Maybe he didn't defend his friends, but I did. "There is when you insult the people I care about. Or is it that anyone who's friends with me must be too stuck up for this part of town? Ignoring the fact that one of them is ecstatic to be getting married practically on your street."

After a silent pause, he shook his head. "You're right. I shouldn't make assumptions about people. But, uh, what did you tell Darnell when he suggested you hire me to renovate the house?"

"I told him no, and you know why. We talked about this already."

"You didn't just tell him no, though. You didn't believe I was qualified to do the work."

Darnell needed to learn to keep his mouth shut. "I didn't know how much experience you had."

Lips pursed, he tilted his head. "So you *assumed* that I didn't have the know-how. Even after he told you I'd flipped other houses, including Hickamore House."

Jaw tight, I said, "Yes."

"Then it looks like we both need to stop making assumptions." He went back to his tacos, clearly content that the conversation was over.

His calm logic only made me more annoyed. Who fought like this? All civilized and rational. It wasn't normal.

"Do you ever get mad about *anything*?" I asked.

Unfazed by the question, he licked salsa off his thumb and I nearly lost focus. "Yeah, but only when I have a good reason."

I had to know. "What's a good reason?"

He wiped his hands on a napkin and looked off into the distance. "If someone threatens or harms the people I care about."

I waited for him to elaborate. He didn't. "That's it?"

"That's the only reason I can think of."

"What about all the injustice in the world? Doesn't it bother you?"

"Something bothering me and me getting mad about it are two different things. I'm not blind. I see the world for what it is, and I affect change the best way I know how. I work to improve my little corner of it, and to make things better for the people around me. That might not seem like much, but it's the only way I know how to be."

The man truly was rational to the core. Realistic, yet hopeful. Surrounded by struggle, yet still sweetly optimistic. How did anyone endure what he had and end up so...nice?

Returning my attention to the food, I shook my head. "You're an enigma, my friend. A carpenter yogi wrapped in a pair of magical overalls. Someone should study you to get answers for the rest of us."

Calvin chuckled. "There's nothing special about me."

On this, we could not agree. "Not true. I'd say you're quite special."

Sappiness entered my body and for once I didn't push it away. When he met my gaze, soft smile curling his full lips, something slid into place. The feeling scared me, but instead of running out the door, which would have been standard operation for me in the past, I stayed put.

As he'd said earlier, I was right where I needed to be.

Chapter Fourteen

I couldn't believe I was about to do this.

"Are you nervous about something?" Calvin asked as we climbed the stairs up to Josie's apartment. I'd hoped he wouldn't notice all the twitching.

"I'm fine," I replied, far too snippy to be true.

Because Josie lived on Mount Washington, which was the prime spot to watch the fourth of July fireworks thanks to the main drag looming high over downtown, we were all gathering for a chill celebration. The baby turned two months old the day before, and Jacob's older daughter Sophie was also tagging along. She adored watching the fireworks right in front of her instead of having to crank her neck to see them high up in the sky.

The kids, of course, didn't bother me. My agitation stemmed from the person beside me. I hadn't brought a man to a friend group gathering in... I couldn't even remember how long. When was the last time I'd even dated? This should not have been a hard answer to come up with, but I had nothing. Either way, this was big for me.

Not that Calvin and I were officially dating. We'd only had the one meal at Rosalie's. But throughout the week since, I found myself coming up with varied, and often thin, excuses to stop by the house.

Not that I didn't get a kick out of watching the place come together, but Calvin was the real reason I kept dropping in unannounced. To his credit, he never mentioned my frequent visits or asked why I was there.

"You don't seem fine." We reached the first landing and turned to take the next set of stairs up to Josie's floor. "Is there something I should know about what we're walking into?"

The last thing I needed was for both of us to be freaked out.

"This is just a casual gathering of my friends. You know them all, though you'll get to see Becca in person this time instead of on a phone screen. And their significant others are here, of course." I was babbling but my mouth and brain had now disengaged. "All but Lindsey, of course. She's the other single one. Other than me."

We finally reached the apartment door and before knocking, I spun to face him, took a deep breath, and confessed the truth.

"The thing is, I haven't brought a...friend around in a long time."

Dark brows furrowed. "These friends don't let you have *other* friends?"

"No, that's not it. A male friend."

Rationally, this statement cleared up nothing, but the more I talked the more pathetic I sounded so I shut up.

Seconds passed until he finally caught on to what I *wasn't* saying. With a broad grin, he nodded. "That kind of a friend. I got you." Calvin looked at the closed door, then back to me. "I'll play this however you want."

Of course, he would. What else would Saint Calvin say? He'd ditched the overalls for jeans and a blue button-up shirt with the sleeves rolled up to his elbows. The Nikes, along with a tiny gold hoop in his left earlobe—which I had never seen before—made the look classy and casual at the same time.

One thought went through my mind. *I'm happy he's here.* I'd never felt that way about anyone, so this was a big revelation. The girls already knew how I felt about him. Why was I making such a big deal of this?

Before I could change my mind, I said, "You're here as my date."

Based on his reaction, I'd taken him by surprise. After rubbing his hands on his thighs, he flexed his shoulders like maybe he planned to carry me over the threshold.

Confused, I said, "You know you aren't carrying me through this door, right?"

"I hadn't planned on it. Not yet, anyway." What did *that* mean? "Should we go in?"

Hit by a sudden urge for a drink, I lifted my hand to knock. My knuckle had barely touched the surface when the door flew open to reveal Megan, Josie, and Lindsey staring back at us with knowing smiles on their faces.

They'd clearly been listening from the other side. "Can you guys not embarrass me right away, please?"

"We make no promises," Josie muttered as she pulled my date into the apartment. "Guys, you have to meet Calvin." She dragged him into the living room with Megan hot on her heels, leaving me standing in the hall.

I turned to Lindsey. "They're going to make this as painful as possible, aren't they?"

"If by painful you mean fawn over your boyfriend and tell all sorts of humiliating stories about you, then yes. Yes, they are."

"He isn't my boyfriend," I said, stepping inside. "Is everyone else here?"

"We're waiting for Becca, Jacob, and the kids. Turns out having a baby requires bringing lots of stuff and makes you late."

We stepped into the living room to see Josie showing Calvin the photo album from Becca's wedding in January. A blizzard blew up out of nowhere that day, nearly preventing the bride from reaching the church, and resulting in all of us looking worse than we'd have liked by the time the ceremony started.

Leaning closer, Lindsey said, "There's wine in the kitchen."

Turning that way, I muttered, "Thank God."

———

"You're really good at that," I said an hour later, taking a seat beside Calvin on the couch. "I think he likes you."

The baby squirmed, stretched, then settled back into the strong hands holding him. Every time I saw him, I marveled at how tiny Noah was. Becca assured me all newborns were this small, but I still couldn't get over it. The itty bitty fingers and toes and the way his limbs seemed to bend like a contortionist.

Watching Calvin hold him so confidently shouldn't have surprised me. Where I was deathly afraid of dropping him, the calm carpenter acted as if he did this every day. Leaning forward, elbows on his knees, he slowly swayed the child back and forth.

"I like kids," he said, eyes on the infant. "And they like me."

So did I.

"Becca said he was fussy earlier. Doesn't seem to be the case now."

He shifted from swaying to lightly bouncing. "My cousins call me the baby whisperer. When they couldn't get their babies to sleep, I'd come over and have them out in no time."

Feeling brave, I asked, "Do you want your own some day?"

Continuing to coo at the infant, he didn't answer right away. When I was about to withdraw the question, he said, "Maybe I can change the pattern from how I grew up, but is maybe good enough?" Calvin looked my way. "Babies shouldn't be guinea pigs, you know?"

What I was about to say had nothing to do with my summersaulting ovaries.

"You'd be a great dad, Calvin. I'm absolutely certain of it."

For the first time ever, I saw doubt in his eyes. "What makes you so sure?"

"You're one of the most selfless, even-keeled people I've ever met. You naturally take care of people. It's your default setting." Reaching out, I let the baby wrap his perfect little hand around my finger. "This little one clearly agrees with me, and I trust his judgment."

"Maybe he's just a really chill baby."

"Not in my experience." I loved the little stinker, but the handful of times I'd gotten to see him, he was always upset about something, and loudly making his feelings known.

Pulling Noah up to his chest, Calvin cradled him in one arm as he leaned back on the couch. "What about you?"

"What about me?"

"You want kids?"

I hadn't considered having the question turned back my way. "I'm on the fence," I said honestly. "Seems cruel to have a kid then say 'By the way, the planet might cough you off before you reach middle age.'"

Calvin nodded. "Good point."

"I didn't like being an only child, so I wouldn't want to have just one, but I'm not getting any younger."

"You didn't like being an only child?" he asked.

Leaning back, I pressed my shoulder to his and stared at my fingers. "I was pretty lonely."

He let that one sit for several seconds before saying, "I'm sorry."

I shifted to look at his face. "Why are you sorry? It wasn't your fault."

"Doesn't mean I can't be sorry. I guess neither of us had a perfect childhood."

The details of his younger years were still a mystery. I understood what he'd left unsaid that day at his house, but only in that something bad happened to him. Did I want to ask? Should I? He'd alluded to his childhood twice now so maybe he was open to the subject.

"This might be none of my business, but what happened back then?"

His deep breath lifted the baby, causing him to squirm. With a soft bounce, he settled the child, then met my gaze.

"Mom was young when she had me, and she wasn't equipped to be a parent. Her parents weren't great, so she didn't know how to be any better. I think she was over-whelmed when I look back on it now. She'd either withdraw entirely, or lash out without warning. Hard to be a kid in that situation."

My heart broke for the little boy he was. "I had no idea."

My only memories were of us all running through the neighborhood when we weren't hanging on this person's porch or that street corner. Calvin had been the natural leader, full of confidence and seemingly more mature than the rest of us. Now I knew why. He had to grow up faster than we did.

His lips curled into a sad smile as he brushed Noah's hair off his forehead. "No one did. I worked hard to keep it that way."

"Why, though? Why not tell so that someone could have helped you?"

"Because help would have meant taking me away. From Mom and the neighborhood. Better to stay where I knew who and what the dangers were, and where I had places I knew were safe. Even if my house wasn't one of them."

My heart broke even more. No kid should have to make that choice. At the same time, that experience made him the person he was today. Empathetic, generous, and kind. So kind. Calvin had beat the odds in every possible way.

"I hate to break this up," Becca said, interrupting our conversation, "but it's feeding time."

He lifted the baby up to her. "Can't have him missing a meal."

Becca kissed her baby's head as she walked off, and Calvin and I sat back in a comfortable silence. As the others around us ate chips and chatted away, I wrapped my pinky around his and whispered, "I'm sorry, too."

Squeezing my finger with his, he whispered back, "Thanks."

———

SINCE THE BABY WAS SLEEPING, Becca stayed at the apartment while the rest of us walked the four blocks down to Grandview for the fireworks show. Sophie bounced along, riding the sugar high from eating too many desserts, with Jacob holding one hand and Lindsey holding the other.

Though Linds taught high school, she was good with kids of any age. Much like Megan, who ran the children's reading program at her library. I'd spent time with Sophie during these gatherings, but we hadn't bonded like she had with the others. She'd recently turned eight, and my busy schedule had kept me from attending her birthday party.

As we squeezed in where we could along the overlook, I felt a pat on my arm. Looking down, I found Sophie's big brown eyes looking up at me.

"Thank you for the camera," she said. "It's really cool."

Not attending didn't mean I hadn't sent a present. What else would a photographer get a little girl than her own camera? This one spit out tiny little Polaroid pictures, and Jacob had given his approval ahead of time for her to have it.

"I'm glad you like it."

"I brought this to show you." She reached into her pocket and pulled out one of the Polaroids. "What do you think? Did I do good?"

Pulling out my phone, I switched on the light to examine the image. Sitting in the bright yellow petal of a flower was a ladybug, just off center. She'd framed it perfectly.

"Sophie, this is really good."

"Really?" she asked, and I realized this was important to her.

I leaned down to her level. "The red on the yellow is a lovely contrast, and you did a great job of making the ladybug the focus while still showing the beauty around it." Handing the picture back, I added, "You've got a talent for taking pictures."

She looked up with a proud smile. "You can keep it if you want."

Straightening, I returned the smile. "I'd like that, thank

you." Happy to foster her interest, I came up with an idea. "Maybe we could visit the botanical gardens one day and I could teach you how to take pics with one of my cameras."

Her eyes went wide. "You'd do that?"

"Sure, but you have to make sure it's okay with your parents."

She jumped for joy, but before she could fully celebrate our potential day out, the first firework of the evening lit up the sky. Though we'd found a rare spot on the railing, Sophie wasn't tall enough to see over the heavy fencing.

Instead of reaching for her father, Sophie tugged on Calvin's shirt. "Pick me up, please!"

He looked to Jacob, who laughed and said, "You don't have to. I can lift her."

Calvin shook his head. "I don't mind." With one quick move, he swept the little one up onto his left shoulder like a stack of lumber. "Can you see?"

Sophie clapped excitedly. "I can!"

Another firework filled the sky and she squealed with glee. The next half hour was filled with lots of booms, countless oohs and aahs, and endless joy from the child perched high above the other onlookers. Halfway through, Jacob offered to take her, but Calvin waved him off. She was comfortable and he didn't appear to be straining at all.

Then again, the beams and tools he carried probably weighed more than Sophie did.

When the show ended, she skipped over to hold hands with Megan and Ryan for the walk back. Little Sophie had no lack with social skills, which reminded me off her mother. Jill had once mentioned how she enjoyed throwing large gatherings while she and Jacob were married, but he'd merely tolerated them.

As we made the walk back, ears ringing and enjoying the light breeze, Calvin slid his hand into mine. I looked over to catch a glimpse of his face in the glow of a streetlight. Without a word, he squeezed my hand, gave me a wink, and continued to walk in silence.

My heart skipped a beat as warmth danced up my cheeks, and in that moment, I knew that nothing would ever be the same again.

Chapter Fifteen

"What are *you* doing here?" I asked when I pulled up in front of the house and found Darnell walking toward me.

He shrugged. "I don't know. Cal called and said I needed to come over."

I received the same message by text. So much for thinking he just wanted to see me. Truth be told, I was happy to have a reason to stop by. Work had been so busy it felt as if this project was happening without me.

As we made our way to the front door, a sense of dread slid up my spine. "I hope this isn't anything bad."

Nothing major had gone wrong so far. In fact, Calvin claimed to be ahead of schedule, which JoJo said *never* happened. She claimed he was pushing them like a madman, paying overtime to anyone who would stay late. I considered letting him know I was fine with whatever condition the house was in when I took up early residence, but part of me kind of wanted a functioning kitchen along with the bathroom.

Selfish, but if the team was willing to work over, who was I to stop them?

When we reached the porch, Calvin stepped out of the house and held up a hand. "You need to walk around back."

My schedule had prevented me from stopping by for more than a week. It had also kept me from seeing Calvin. We sent texts every day, but despite my constant requests, he refused to send me pictures of the house. If I pushed hard enough, he'd send me something like a hammer on the floor.

"Why can't we go inside?" I asked.

"Floors are going down."

I was pretty sure the floors had gone down earlier in the month. "The floors were supposed to be done by now."

"They're going in today."

Smelling a rat, I stared into his eyes trying to determine if he was telling the truth. The man was stone cold. He must have been really good at poker.

"Why are we here?" Darnell asked.

"We found a few things while putting the posts in for the deck." He stepped between us and led the way through the narrow side yard.

The addition was fully built and closed in. Windows were in and all that appeared to be missing was the siding. As we rounded the corner, an overwhelming mix of awe and pride brought tears to my eyes. I'd pictured this in my head a thousand times, but to see it for real. To see my dream literally coming to life tightened every muscle in my chest.

"These were buried in three different places in the yard,"

Calvin said, drawing my attention away from the looming addition. As I joined them at the deck, he said, "After finding the first two, we brought in a metal detector to see if there were any more. That's when we found the third one. Have either of you seen these before?"

Three metal boxes, rusted and half covered in mud, sat in a row on the deck. They were rectangular, about three or four inches tall, and not quite a foot long.

"They don't look familiar to me." I looked to Darnell. "How about you?"

He shook his head. "I've never seen them either. They look older than we are, so I bet they were buried before we were born. What's in them?"

Calvin crossed his arms. "That's what you're here to find out. Since Donna owns the land, whatever is in these things belongs to her, but it felt like you both should be here to open them."

If Pops put these in the ground, then whatever was inside didn't only belong to me. "You want to go first?" I asked Darnell.

"Let's open a couple at the same time." I could tell he had the same Christmas morning feeling that I did.

What were we going to find? Time capsules? Pictures or trinkets from previous generations of the family? We didn't have much family history beyond Pops and Bammy's parents, all of whom were born in the south and migrated north after the war in search of a better life than what they could get in Mississippi and Alabama.

Somehow both families had landed in Pittsburgh, allowing Bammy and Pops to meet, and making it possible for both me and Darnell to exist. Amazing how many pieces had to fall into place for us to be in the world at all.

There were no locks on the boxes, but the latches were nearly rusted shut. Calvin handed us each a screwdriver to pry them open. Once the latches both gave way, Darnell counted down and we each lifted a lid at the same time.

And both stood in stunned silence.

Calvin leaned forward when neither of us spoke. "What is it?"

"Money," I said.

"A lot of money," Darnell added, pulling a stack from his box. "Looks like tens and twenties."

I lifted my stack and carefully scanned the bills. "Dar, these are hundreds."

He quickly reached for the other box, prying the latch in seconds and flipping open the lid. "There's more hundreds in here." Withdrawing the treasure, he looked at me with eyes wide. "Why did Pops bury this money? Mom has talked about times being tight back in the day. This makes no sense."

"Are you sure it was him?" Calvin asked. "What's the dates on the bills?"

We each took a closer look at the money. "Mine are all in the seventies."

"Same here," said Darnell. "Definitely Pops."

We needed input from someone who knew more than we did. "Let me call Dad."

With a few swipes on my phone, I had him on the line and put him on speaker. "Dad, I'm at the house with Darnell and Calvin. Do you know anything about Pops burying money in the backyard?"

"Money?" he repeated, sounding as shocked as we were. "You found money?"

"Calvin's crew did," I explained. "We haven't counted it yet, but there are three metal boxes with a large stack of bills in each. A couple of them have hundred dollar bills."

"What the..." he trailed off. Seconds later, Dad burst out laughing and the three of us stared at each other in confusion.

"Dad, what's so funny?"

Once he regained control, he said, "That explains so much."

"Explains what?" Darnell asked.

"A couple of times a year, Pops would go out and dig a hole in the backyard. I asked Mom once what he was doing and she said, 'Trying to dig his way out of a divorce.'" Dad started laughing again. "I always wondered what she meant. Now we know."

"She knew," I whispered, thinking of all the years she'd made a dollar stretch farther than anyone I'd ever met. "They never told you this was out here?"

"No one told me," Dad replied. "Dar, you need to ask your mom. She might have known, but if she did, then so would everyone else. So I'm guessing none of us knew."

Aunt Jackie was the gossip in the family. No way would she have kept something like this to herself.

"She's at work, but I'll ask when she gets off." As a nurse at the local children's hospital, Aunt Jackie didn't like getting calls during working hours. This might be an exception to the rule, though.

Still amused, Dad said, "Let me know how much it is

once you count it. This'll be a fun story at the next family cookout."

This was more than a fun story. This was real money. Found in my backyard.

"What should we do with it?" I asked.

"It's your money. You bought the house, so you get whatever comes with it."

That didn't seem fair. Dad and his siblings had gone without because Pops had been crazy enough to bury what looked to be a lot of money. Money that would have gone even farther back then than it would now.

"But this is yours and Aunt Jackie's."

Dad was not swayed. "Use it for the house. That's what it should have gone for anyway. I don't know how many times something broke and Mom would duct tape it or tie a string around it or tell us just not to use it. All while mumbling about that worthless man and his damn shovel. Another mystery statement solved."

I looked to Darnell, brows arched in question.

"I'm good with that," he said. "The money belongs here." Turning to Calvin, he said, "Just do something nice with it."

"I'll do whatever Donna wants."

Feeling as if I'd been handed a great deal of power, I rubbed my forehead. "We'll see once we've counted it. I'm not sure it's right for me to keep all of it."

"Then let's head up to the porch and count it," Calvin suggested.

"Why can't we go inside and do it?"

"The floors—"

"—are going in," I finished. "You're a terrible liar, you know that?"

"I'm not lying." Again, he offered no readable facial expression.

More curious about the buried treasure, I let the topic go. "Fine. Then we'll count it on the porch."

———

MY BRAIN COULD HARDLY PROCESS what we'd just discovered. "Three thousand dollars."

"Three thousand four hundred and eighty-five to be exact." Darnell laughed as if this was all a joke. "Imagine how much Bammy could have done with this money."

Calvin pulled out his phone. "Let's see what three thousand in the seventies means in today's money." A few swipes later he let out a long whistle. "Over twenty-eight thousand dollars. Holy moly."

"That would have been life changing money for them." I closed the lid on the box in front of me. "What was Pops thinking?"

"He was thinking he didn't trust the banks." Calvin closed the other two boxes. "The real question is, how do you want to spend it?"

My gut said this wasn't my money to spend, but Dad and Darnell had a point about the funds going toward the house.

"Do you think Aunt Jackie will want some?" I asked Darnell.

"Ma will tell you the same thing me and Uncle Ronnie did. Use it for the house." He rose off the milk crate he'd been using as a seat. "Totally worth cutting out early on that pickup game. I can't wait to tell Tiff. She's not gonna believe it."

As he stepped off the porch, I said, "Hey, have Aunt Jackie call me." Regardless of his assumption, I still wanted to talk to her directly before making any decisions.

"Will do," my cousin replied as he strolled up the sidewalk.

From my own milk crate, I stared at the boxes as if they might explode. Bammy's life could have been so much easier. She'd never complained, and had always made the most of what she did have, but what a difference this would have made.

All I wanted was to turn back time. To go back and give her the money so she could do whatever she wanted with it.

"She'd want you to have it," Calvin said, reading my mind. "You're the only one who loves this house as much as she did."

Overwhelmed, I dropped my head into my hands. "I wish she was here to tell me what to do."

A warm hand squeezed my shoulder. "You're doing great. The house is coming back to life because of you."

He was giving me too much credit. "You're doing all the work."

"You helped take down that wall."

I should be doing more. Not the heavy lifting, of course, but more than a little demo and painting my own bedroom. "I'm sorry I haven't been around. I'm taking every extra job that comes my way in case we need more in the contingency fund."

"Donna, you don't need to worry about the budget. The foundation is good. The house is level." He ticked each item off on a finger. "We've had heavy storms and there's been no water issues in the basement. The termite test came up negative. You don't have anything to worry about."

The renovation wasn't my only source of stress. I still needed to pack up my apartment and studio, and I still didn't know if I would be able to run the business out of the house yet.

"What about the zoning? Do we know yet if I can have a studio upstairs?"

Calvin offered a half grin. "I was going to surprise you with that one."

Bolting to my feet, I nearly pulled him up by his overalls. "Have you been holding out on me?"

He took his time getting to his feet and it was all I could do not to shake the answer out of him. Once upright, he slid his hands into his pockets. "I got the letter this morning. You're all clear for the studio."

The sudden news stunned me for a good five seconds before I yelled, "Holy crap!" Then, without thinking, I grabbed his face with both hands and dropped a loud kiss of joy on his full lips. The moment I pulled back, I realized what I'd done. "I'm so sorry. I shouldn't have done that."

Pink danced along his cheeks as his smile widened. "Remind me to give you good news more often."

Now I was blushing.

"I need to go upstairs and map out where I want everything."

Before I could step around him, Calvin cut me off. "You can't go inside."

"Why not?"

"You just can't."

This was my house, so... "I want to go look at the studio."

"I told you. The floors—"

"Calvin Hopkins, if you lie about those floors one more time."

He had the nerve to roll his eyes. "Okay, fine. The floors are done, but you still can't go in."

What the heck was he up to? Reality set in. They weren't ahead of schedule at all. The place probably wasn't even halfway done.

"You do know I'm moving in the last week of August. That's five weeks from now."

"The twenty-sixth. I know."

"So I'm going to see the place no matter what it looks like at that point."

Calvin nodded.

I considered my options. If I really pushed, what would he do? What could he do? Would he physically keep me out? Carry me to my car? The thought sent a zing down my spine, which I ignored. Then I remembered I had a key. I could come back tonight and he'd never know.

Relaxing, I shrugged. "Fine. You win." I turned to collect the metal boxes. "Let me know when I'm permitted access again."

"Donna."

Shoving a box under my arm, I pretended that him saying my name in that sultry tone had no effect on me. "Hm?"

Calvin spun me around with one finger on my arm. "Please don't come by when I'm not here."

Dang it. He really could read my mind. With him flashing those puppy dog eyes, how was I supposed to sneak in behind his back and not feel horrible about it? The curiosity was killing me.

"I agreed to stay out of the way. I never agreed to stay out *entirely*." Resorting to whining, I pushed out my lower lip like a toddler. "Why can't I go in?"

"Just give me a week, then you can walk through the whole thing."

That didn't seem like too much to ask. I was mostly booked for the next week anyway. Hugging all three boxes to my chest, I accepted my fate. "Fine. A week. But I'm coming back next Friday, and I *will* be going inside. Agreed?"

"Agreed." Calvin caught one of the boxes as it fell. "I'll help you get these to the car. What are you going to do with them?"

"Take them to the bank, I guess. I'll deposit the money into my savings until I can talk to Aunt Jackie." I needed her approval before spending anything. Regardless of who owned the land, this was hers and Dad's before it was mine.

"If she says the same thing your dad did, we can talk about options." He opened my passenger door and stepped back so I could drop the boxes. "You'll need to decide soon, though, so we can work the changes into the project."

Based on the initial timeline, there was three months of work left. That seemed like lots of time to decide how to use the money. Then again, he was the expert. If Calvin said we needed to decide soon then I wouldn't argue.

"I'll think about it and try to have an answer next week."

I turned around to find very little space between his body and mine. When Calvin leaned forward to place the third box on the seat, he was so close I forgot to breathe. Deep brown eyes lingered on my lips for several seconds and I attempted to swallow my heart back into my chest.

"Waiting a week to see the house doesn't mean we can't see each other before that," he said.

Picturing my calendar in my head, I said, "I'm free Tuesday night."

"I'll pick you up at six?"

Mouth dry, I nodded my agreement. The affect this man had on me was getting scary.

He stepped back and I nearly followed. "See you then." That grin would be my undoing, if the rest of him didn't shatter me first.

I nodded again and could see that he was enjoying this a little too much. Clearing my throat, I closed the car door and walked around to the other side. Digging deep for my non-existent swagger, I said, "Don't be late."

"Oh, I won't," he said with a salute.

How did he manage to be smug and cute at the same time? My heart beat like a drum for several blocks, long after I'd lost sight of him in the rearview mirror. Were we really doing this? That impromptu kiss had been nice. I wouldn't mind doing *that* again. And again.

"Woman, you have got to get a grip," I said to my empty car. Looking down at the money boxes, I mumbled, "Now to figure out what to do with you."

Chapter Sixteen

Sunday morning, we skipped our breakfast meet up to gather at Becca's place to work on Megan's wedding. Becca had been easing back into work over the last few weeks, and she certainly didn't need our help, but Megan wanted to include all of us since we were all bridesmaids.

Her half-sister, Cassie O'Malley—who she discovered only two years ago—was the maid of honor, but she was a college student out of town for the summer and not able to join us in person. Megan included her through a video call, but she'd had to go after a half hour on the phone. Something about hiking and losing signal. As a devoted city girl, I did not see the attraction in climbing rocks or walking in ugly boots through dirt and trees.

But, to each her own.

Most of our meet ups had been held at Becca's since the baby arrived. There was no reason to make her pack up Noah and come to us when we could go to her. The one time we all met for lunch, she'd left him with her mom and the rest of us whined about not getting our baby time. That made the location for future gatherings an obvious choice.

"I just don't like the idea of dragging my dress halfway up my thigh so a man can remove an elastic band that serves no purpose." Megan's perfect little nose scrunched with distaste. "I get that it's tradition, but I'm not doing it."

"You don't have to do anything you don't want to," Becca assured her. "So we're a go with the ceremony outside, and then everyone moves into the banquet hall. This means we won't need the upstairs bar for cocktails in between, since they can have the reception set up and ready for guests immediately."

"I like that better," Megan said, swaying back and forth as she held Noah. "Not that the bar upstairs isn't beautiful, but we aren't cocktail party people. I want guests to feel relaxed and to enjoy the food and dancing right after the ceremony."

"What about the pictures?" I asked. "If we do them before the ceremony, Ryan will see you in your dress."

"That would be bad luck," Josie said.

Lindsey scoffed. "That's a superstition that needs to go along with the garter crap."

Megan looked conflicted. "I don't know. I'd rather not tempt fate. Can we offer hors d'oeuvres during the pictures?"

Becca tapped the pen on her notepad. "We can do anything you want. I'll add that to the caterer's schedule, and we'll take the pictures right after the ceremony while the guests are getting settled in the hall."

I needed to scope out picture locations so we wouldn't be wandering around the day of trying to find the right spots.

Since I had an in with the guy who ran the place, I'd set up another visit.

Yes, I was in the wedding, but I had no intention of letting someone else shoot those all-important pictures. Another photographer had been hired to handle the ceremony and reception, but I was handling the ones in between.

"We can knock them out pretty quickly once I map out the locations."

"I trust you," the bride said, handing the sleeping baby off to Josie. "Though I'd really like one in that gazebo. And the library. Oh, I wonder if we can get into the Speakeasy room?"

Those were all locations I'd already considered. "I'm way ahead of you."

The next fifteen minutes were spent discussing the menu, and the program for the DJ to follow. Wedding party entrance, food, the bouquet toss—because some traditions were worth keeping—and the cutting of the cake. Then the party would kick off in full force.

Becca set the notepad and pen on the coffee table. "I'll pass all of this on to Amanda for finalizing. Don't forget about the fittings on Tuesday. We meet at the dress shop at five thirty."

Oh crap. "I thought that was on Thursday."

"No, it's Tuesday. Didn't you put it on your calendar?"

Checking my phone, I pulled up the week ahead and there it was. Five thirty on Tuesday. *Dress fitting.*

"Can we move just mine? I made plans for six o'clock."

"Are you doing a late session?" Josie asked.

If it was work, they'd let me off the hook, but I couldn't lie. "No, I have a date."

"With Calvin?" Megan asked.

"Yeah. I'm really sorry. He asked me to dinner and my brain glitched and I said I was free on Tuesday." Feeling like a jerk for putting a man before my friends, especially when it was something for the wedding, I took back my request. "I'll tell him we have to go a different night."

Becca looked at Megan. "It's up to you. I can move her appointment with no problem."

"Let her go," Lindsey said. "We've all seen how good he is for her. She deserves this."

Where did that come from? "What do you mean he's *good* for me?"

The baby started to fuss so Josie rose to her feet and walked him around, bouncing as she went. "You can't pretend you don't see it."

"See what?"

"How he makes your life easier," Megan said.

The man was renovating my house. Whatever contractor I'd hired would have done the same. It's not as if I'd planned to do it myself before Calvin came to my rescue.

"He's doing a job I'm paying him to do. How is that making my life easier?"

"He's done more than that," Becca said. "Like help get your car fixed. Fought for that permit so you can have a studio in the house."

"Came up with the French doors idea," Lindsey continued. "Bent over backwards to make the house *exactly* how you want it."

Focusing on the last statement, I said, "That's what I'm paying him to do."

"Don't you remember all those other contractors? The ones who wanted to charge too much or claimed that what you wanted couldn't be done?" Josie made a lap around the kitchen island while shifting the baby up onto her shoulder. "Has Calvin said no to *any* of your requests? Heck, he even found you money you didn't know was there. Some contractors might have walked off with those boxes and you'd never have known."

We'd talked about the buried money when I'd first arrived. My conversation with Aunt Jackie the day before hadn't taken long. She'd laughed as Dad had, and told me the same thing. The money was mine.

"I doubt all other contractors are criminals."

"Not all," Lindsey said, "but she's right. Calvin not only didn't keep it, he brought in a metal detector to make sure they didn't miss anything." Brows arched, she added, "He did that for you. That man would do *anything for you.*"

The conversation with Mom and Dad replayed in my head. I wanted a man who would make my life easier, not harder. With every fiber of my being, I thought that would never happen. Calvin definitely challenged me at times, but he also made my life easier in countless ways.

I stared at the toes of my Nike sneakers. How did my friends notice this when I didn't? And how was the most perfect guy I'd ever met still available after all these years? More importantly, what was I going to do with him?

"I'm rescheduling Donna's fitting, then?" Becca asked.

"Yes," the other three said in unison.

Annoyed, I crossed my arms. "Don't I get a say?"

"You already asked if we could move it," Becca reminded

her. "I'll make the call first thing in the morning. I assume you're free on Thursday at the same time?"

I quickly checked my calendar again to be sure. "Yes."

She reached to the coffee table to make the note. "That's settled then. Now it's time for little man to eat."

"Speaking of your house," Lindsey said, "when will the renovations be finished? Aren't you moving in soon?"

"I move in the last week of August, but the completion date is still up in the air. Calvin tells me it's on schedule, but that's all I know. Early on, he mentioned middle of October, so I'm not expecting to have the house to myself until then."

Buying the house had taken ten years, and I planned to live there for the rest of my life. What was a few months of construction if the result meant having the house exactly how I wanted it?

I couldn't get past the do anything for me comment. Was that true, or would he go above and beyond for any client? His business depended upon creating happy customers who would either give him a good review or recommend him to others. Preferably both.

Yes, we were casually seeing each other outside of the project and we had a history. But they were making some major assumptions about a guy they barely knew. I didn't remember any of them spending a ton of time with him on the fourth. At least not without me around.

They were seeing what they wanted to see because they wanted me to be happy. Maybe I could be happy with Calvin, but part of me said don't get too excited. There was still a chance that once the house was finished we'd go our separate ways, and then I'd rarely see him outside of neighborhood events.

The thought made me grumpy, which was all the more reason to rein this romance-y stuff in now, before I lost my head entirely. Did I like Calvin? Yes. Did Calvin seem to like me? Yes. Were we on our way to a happily ever after like what my friends had recently found?

The jury was still out on that one.

"Living in a construction zone for that long is going to suck." Lindsey passed Becca a burping cloth from the end table beside her. "How far along are they right now?"

Another good question. "I don't know. I've been too busy to check in much, and Calvin wouldn't let me go inside the day he gave me the money boxes."

"Wouldn't let you go inside? I don't know if I want to hire him if he does that." Megan and Ryan had decided planning a wedding was enough stress for one year and put off the house hunting until next spring. They were still determined to find a fixer-upper.

"Maybe he doesn't want clients to freak out when things are only half done," I said, defending him. "I'd be worried if I walked in to find wires hanging from the ceiling and walls still half open."

The work had been in full swing for only three months. This project was more than making a few cosmetic changes. The renovations were major, and knowing how much the house mattered to me, I could understand him not wanting me to see it in rougher shape than how I found it.

"He said I can go in on Friday so I'll let you know what I find. So long as I can see it coming together, I'll be happy."

"We expect a full report," Josie said, taking a seat beside Lindsey on the loveseat. "On the house *and* the date."

There likely wouldn't be much to say about either. "Yinz need to lower your expectations on the date part. This is just casual for now."

"For now," Lindsey repeated, exchanging a glance with the others,.

Arguing with them would get me nowhere so I held my tongue and let the discussion roll on to other topics. Ones that had nothing to do with my love life, or lack thereof.

———

I WAS NEVER GOING to forgive them for this.

For two days, I'd been a nervous wreck. One minute everything was in perspective. Calvin and I were spending time together. No big deal. The next minute words like *forever* and *in love* and *my person* bounced around in my head.

The girls had planted these seeds, and I was the one choking on them.

I couldn't even call them for a sanity check, since they were all at the dress fitting. Technically, this would have been a good time to get them on the phone all at the same time, but I wouldn't ruin their evening by making it about me. Skipping out on them was bad enough.

I should have rescheduled the date. Or canceled it entirely. What was the point? Nothing was going to come of this, just as nothing had ever come of any of my relationships.

Not that Calvin and I were in a relationship. We could be. Maybe. Eventually. But not likely.

The buzzer letting me know he was downstairs went off and I froze in place.

Did I buzz him in and let him come up, or should I meet him downstairs? I'd stayed up late the night before cleaning every inch of the apartment down to the baseboards just in case he did come in. Because *that's* what a man checked out when he visited a woman's apartment for the first time.

Her baseboards.

Seconds ticked by as I debated what to do. Finally, I grabbed my purse, tossed my keys inside, and locked the door behind me. My apartment was on the second floor so I took the stairs instead of waiting for the elevator. In the building foyer, I spotted Calvin through the thick glass door.

Butterflies burst to life in my stomach. Before Sunday, I saw this dinner as a fun opportunity to spend time with a guy I liked. Now I felt almost annoyed. Like he'd snuck up on me when I wasn't looking and attempted to swipe my heart right out of my chest.

Who said he could do that?

"Hi there," he said as I stepped through the door. "You look good."

This was the fourth outfit I'd put on, and the only reason I stuck with the dark jeans, burgundy off the shoulder top, and knee-high boots was because with every change I grew more annoyed with myself. I'd also run out of time to try another.

"Thanks, you too."

His dress shirt was a similar shade of burgundy and

showed off his broad shoulders to perfection. Adding his dark jeans, we looked as if we'd planned our outfits together. A sudden urge to run back upstairs and change overwhelmed me. A sure sign of my growing insanity.

"Where are we going?" I asked, more snippy than necessary.

"I made a reservation at Kyoto Grill since you mentioned you like Japanese."

"When did I mention that?"

"A few weeks ago."

He remembered an off-handed comment I made weeks ago and took that into consideration for our date. A man who listened, remembered, and took action? There was no way.

I tugged my purse onto my shoulder and offered the best version of a smile I could muster. "Sounds good."

"Are you okay?" he asked, astute as ever. "If you want something else, we can do that. We might have to wait for a table, though."

"No, Japanese is fine. I'm fine. Everything is fine."

Was it? Because I did not sound fine.

Calvin watched me with concern. "You're sure?"

Teeth locked, I nodded. "Where did you park?" The big white truck was nowhere to be seen.

"Right here." He stepped off the curb next to a black sedan and opened the passenger door.

The loose tether holding my nerves together frayed to a dangerous degree. "That's a Mercedes."

With impressive patience, he said, "Yes, it is."

"You have a Mercedes."

"Yes, I do."

"But, what about the truck?"

"My work truck? You'd rather go on a date in my *work truck?*"

If I didn't get a grip, this man was never going to talk to me again, let alone want to go out with me. And as freaked out as I was, that was something I wanted him to keep doing.

"No," I said, sounding as rational as possible. "I guess I thought the truck is what you drive all the time."

He leaned an arm along the top of the door. "You've only ever seen me at work so that makes sense. I bought this about six years ago. She isn't new but thanks to German engineering, she still runs like it."

I had no doubt the car ran beautifully. Owning a luxury car wasn't on my to-do list, but that didn't mean I couldn't appreciate a well-made machine. Which seemed like a good way to describe the car's owner, as well.

Very well made.

Relaxing, I stepped around him and settled into the passenger seat. Dark tan leather eased beneath me, soft and welcoming, and I reached for the seat belt while Calvin walked around to the other side. Admiring the streamlined dash and pretty wood accents, I attempted to ground myself in reality.

We were two old friends getting to know each other again. Spending time with a man who made me feel seen and heard wasn't the worst way to pass an evening. So long as I kept that in mind, whatever was happening here couldn't get too far off the rails.

Chapter Seventeen

"You really do look nice," I said as he buckled in.

"I'm glad you think so. I haven't dressed for a date in a long time. This is the third shirt I put on." Motioning with his thumb to the back seat, he added, "My sport coat is back there because I was sweating too much to put it on."

Knowing I wasn't the only one nervous helped a lot. "I didn't think you had it in you."

"Had what in me?" he asked as we rolled into motion.

"The ability to get nervous. You're always so calm and unaffected."

Calvin kept his eyes straight ahead. "Growing up in chaos teaches you to regulate your emotions. Or so I read somewhere."

Tiptoeing into the topic, I asked, "Do you have any good memories? Any moments when you got to relax and be a kid?"

His blinker ticked as old school R&B played softly from the radio. "Some. A couple times Mom went to rehab we landed with Great-Aunt Tina. She lived on the edge of town down in Canonsburg, in an area where the nearest neighbors were maybe a quarter mile away. I was so used to houses being on top of each other and playing in the streets that having that much dirt and grass to run on took some getting used to."

"How old were you?"

He tilted his head in thought. "Around six the first time, and close to nine the second."

In my memories, he was always around when I stayed at Bammy's. Always part of the crowd, though maybe we weren't out running around that young. Surely not at six, but at nine I know there were days all the kids gathered for freeze tag or kick the can.

"I don't remember you ever being gone."

"I doubt you would have when we were six, but the later stay happened in the winter. Right after Christmas. There probably wasn't much happening where you'd have a reason to miss me."

Doing the math, I figured out what year that would have been and struggled to remember any detail from the time.

"Trevor's birthday," I said.

Calvin brought the car to a stop at a light along Carson Street. "Trevor Stockton?"

"Yes. That was the year he had a birthday party at the skate rink and you weren't there." The memory was so vivid. "I kept asking and no one would tell me where you went."

Brown eyes cut my way. "You remember that?"

"Not until just now. Mrs. Drummond finally told me you were visiting family, but you'd be back soon."

"I didn't think anyone noticed."

"I did." Maybe I'd instinctively known more than I realized. The memory of being worried about him felt as real as if I was experiencing the feeling right then. "I'm glad you came back, but at the same time, I'm sorry you had to. If that makes sense."

Calvin's warm hand settled on mine and our fingers intertwined. "I'm glad I came back, too."

As if by osmosis, his calm seeped into my body and all the nerves went away. We rode in silence, his thumb sliding gently over the back of my hand, and a new word came to mind.

Safe.

With Calvin, I would always be safe. How could that ever be a bad thing?

———

By the time our food came, I'd shared all the dress pics the girls sent to my phone, set up a time to put eyes on this mysterious Speakeasy room, and lost a debate about which of our high schools was better. Calvin had valid points, and in the end I had to admit their indoor pool surpassed our cafeteria coffee bar, but not by much.

Though he was less familiar with Japanese cuisine, Calvin was game to try new things. Not that his marinated beef tips were all that adventurous, but I'd ordered fresh shrimp caramelized with ginger and he didn't hesitate when I offered a bite. He'd also tasted the spicy edamame appetizer I picked, which led him to down his entire glass of water. But still. He'd tried the dish despite stating that he didn't like spicy foods, and I appreciated that.

"Can I ask you a question?" he said.

"You just did."

He arched a brow. "Seriously. Have your parents changed their minds about you buying the house? I expected your dad to want to come see the progress."

I reached for my wine glass. "We're still avoiding the subject. I think once they see it done they'll change their minds. I hope so, anyway. If not, that's less entertaining I have to do."

Realistically, I knew they'd eventually come see the house and be impressed with what we did to it, but that didn't mean they'd change their opinion on whether I should have bought it at all. In their minds, Bammy's neighborhood wasn't worth investing in, and that made me sad.

"Let him know. I'd be happy to show him around," Calvin said. "Maybe seeing it will change his mind."

There he went again trying to make my life easier. The house was the fixer-upper, not me.

"If someone asked you to describe me, what would you say?"

He stopped the process of cutting his steak to give me a questioning look. "You mean what you look like?"

Shaking my head, I set down my fork and sat back. "No, me as a person. How do you see me *as a person?*"

The fact that he took his time before answering proved he was a smarter man than most. I wasn't one to give tests, but if Calvin saw me as some charity case, incapable of handling my own life, then we wouldn't be taking this any further.

Setting down his own silverware, he wiped his mouth on his napkin. "You're smart, ambitious, independent, and surprisingly sentimental. A woman who knows what she wants and goes after it."

Not a bad answer. "That's—"

"You're also stubborn as hell," he added, cutting me off, "and overly defensive."

He should have stopped while he was ahead. "Anything else?"

"That's enough for now."

"For now?"

Pointing at my plate with his knife, he struggled to hide his grin. "Your shrimp is getting cold." Making a well-timed subject change, he asked, "Have you thought about what to do with the extra cash?"

Since his description didn't include damsel in distress or incompetent, I saw no reason not to move on. *For now.* But since talking with the girls on Sunday, I'd been too preoccupied with this date and the man across from me to think about the money.

"Not yet. Do you have any ideas?"

Calvin finished chewing a bite of steak before answering. "How do you feel about built-ins?"

"I'm open to them. Where?"

"Around the fireplace."

The TV would be mounted above the fireplace, both due to the room being too small to put it anywhere else, and because I wanted to keep the mantel as the focal point. Shelves on each side could set it off nicely.

"That would be a good way to display some of the

pictures found in the attic." I already knew I wanted those featured somewhere, but hadn't decided how to do it.

"We can also upgrade your new closet. You picked out a basic design, but with the extra money, we can take that up a notch."

The man was speaking my language. "You've put thought into this, haven't you?"

He shrugged in his typical *it's nothing* way. "I'm your contractor. I need to be ready if and when you ask for my input."

Feeling brave, I tested the waters. "Are you just my contractor?" For him, this could be nothing more than a couple of friends sharing a meal. I needed to know where I stood.

Calvin picked up his wine and swirled the dark liquid around the glass. "That's up to you."

Not an answer. "Do you *want* to be more than just my contractor?"

He set the wine down and clasped his hands in front of his face, elbows on the table. "I've liked you since I was thirteen years old, Donna. Yeah, I *want* to be more than just your contractor. The question is, what do you want?"

This was typically where I'd toss out a snide comment, slam my walls into place, and make a run for it. Only I didn't want to do that. Not this time. Which scared me more than anything.

"I liked you, too," I blurted out.

Calvin's brow furrowed. "You what?"

"Back then. I liked you, too."

By his reaction, this was a shock. "In middle school? You liked me?"

Nodding, I sighed. "All the way into high school. I must have written my name as Donna Hopkins about a thousand times in my notebook."

Jerking back, disbelief covered his face. "You did not."

"I did too."

"I... Why didn't you tell me?"

"Why didn't *you* tell *me*?"

He crossed his arms. "I thought you couldn't stand me."

I cut into a shrimp hard enough to scratch the plate. "I thought you couldn't stand me."

Seconds passed in silence until Calvin started to chuckle, then roll into a full laugh. "We're idiots."

"Hey, speak for yourself," I said, but his laughter was infectious. "We were kids, that's all. Clueless kids."

"We weren't kids that day we measured for your deck. I confessed my old crush, but you didn't mention yours." He loaded a bite onto his fork. "Not cool to leave me hanging like that."

Confessing wasn't my strong suit. "As you said earlier, I'm stubborn as hell, remember? I wasn't ready to come clean that day."

"And now?" he said, watching me.

"Now what? I just admitted I liked you."

"Liked? As in used to but not anymore?"

Oh, that's what he was asking. "Liked as in I liked you back then, and then I didn't like you for a long time, and now I like you again."

His satisfaction was obvious. "Was that so hard?"

"Yes."

Calvin laughed again. "To think. We could have been an old married couple by now."

Time to reel this back in. "There's no way to know that. We probably would have broken up by the end of high school and never spoken again."

After setting his utensils on the plate he pushed it away. "Do you really believe that?"

This time I was taking the fifth. "Where are you taking me for dessert?"

"What do you want?"

Thankfully, my mouth was full so I couldn't slip and say the first thing that came to mind.

Around a bite of shrimp, I said, "How about ice cream?"

He moved the napkin from his lap to the table. "We can do that."

———

THE NIGHT ENDED MUCH DIFFERENTLY than how it started. The ice cream shop was only a block from the restaurant so we'd walked down, hand in hand like the real couple we were quickly becoming. When he first took my hand, my body tensed, but then he gave it a squeeze and flashed me a smile, knowing exactly how to calm me.

Within half a block, I'd relaxed completely. His palm against mine felt right, as if he always should have been there beside me. I wasn't ready to contemplate a happily ever after, but this was nice. Comfortable. So I did my best to let the doubts and fears go. The faint echo of panic danced at the back of my brain, ever present and ready to trigger my flight mode. Shutting that down was going to take more than one dinner date.

This was still progress, and that was enough for now.

"Did you have a good time?" he asked as we made our way back to the car at a leisurely pace.

The night was warm and the scent of kabobs floated around us as we passed one of my favorite Lebanese restaurants. "I did. Thank you for dinner and the ice cream. I'll have to do an extra hour on the treadmill this week, but it was totally worth it."

"You're welcome. That's one plus about working construction. Keeps me in shape." Calvin patted his stomach. "I'll move a few extra two by fours this week to work off that double chocolate crunch."

"I still can't believe you ate that whole thing." He'd ordered the biggest sized cone they had. "How are you not sick right now?"

"Iron gut," he replied. "Been that way since I was a kid. When Mom was out of it, I'd have to make dinner from whatever I could find in the house. You don't want to know some of the stuff I threw together."

"At what age was that?"

He looked off in the distance. "Started around Kindergarten, I guess."

I stopped walking, which pulled him to a halt. "You were making your own dinner when you were five?"

"A kid has to eat." He tugged me back into motion. "Don't start feeling sorry for me. It is what it is. I survived."

I may not have been the warm and fuzzy type, but I still

had a heart, and thinking about Calvin as a little boy, hungry and desperately digging through a likely empty pantry, made me sad and furious at the same time.

"You deserved better," I offered, aware that he wouldn't appreciate my pity.

"That might be true, but I learned to take care of myself and I've been doing it ever since. That's not such a bad thing."

Yes, it was. No child should have to learn that lesson so early.

"Does that mean you're a good cook now?" I asked.

His grip on my hand loosened and I sensed the tension leave his body. "I know my way around a kitchen."

Without thinking, I said, "Good. Then I won't have to do all the cooking."

He turned my way. "You won't have to do all the cooking when?"

Dang it. How did I let that slip? "Just... You know. In the future."

"So we have a future?"

Not much of one if he kept poking at me. "I already admitted I like you. Don't get pushy."

Calvin kissed the back of my hand. "I like you, too."

If his aim was to make me a puddle on the sidewalk, he was doing a fine job of it. Time to change the subject.

"I meant to ask you, how much of my furniture can I bring when I move in? Just the bedroom, right?"

The tension returned. "We'll take a look at that once we get closer to the date."

Was he still bothered that I was moving in early? "I told

you I'll stay out of the way. I won't even be there most of the time."

"We'll make it work." He pressed the key fob to unlock the doors as we approached the car. "Don't worry about it."

He was the one who seemed worried. "I'm not worried."

"That's good." Calvin opened the passenger door, then stepped back. As we'd done at the start of the night, he went around the car as I buckled in. Once inside, he said, "Is there anything else you want to do?"

I checked the time on the center screen. "I have an early appointment so it's a little late to do anything else."

Nine o'clock wasn't late, but I was learning how to read him. Something shifted when I asked about my furniture, and if I pushed the topic, there was a chance the night would end with a fight. Conflict didn't bother me, but in this case there was a danger of undoing the progress we'd made.

Giving him an opening, I said, "Are we good?"

The Mercedes slid into gear and he checked the side mirror before pulling away from the curb. "Yeah, why?"

The chill coming from his side of the car was why, but if he wasn't ready to let me in, I wouldn't push.

"Nothing," I said, focusing on the lights outside my window. "Forget I asked."

Calvin didn't reply and we made the drive to my house in silence. Thankfully, my building wasn't far. When we arrived, he parked in the same space as before, and though I expected a brief goodbye, he opened his door and came around to open mine.

Still in silence, we walked to the large glass door and I pulled out my key card. "Thanks again for dinner."

"Thanks for going with me. I had a good time."

This felt as if we were back in middle school and neither of us knew what to do next. Screw that. I wasn't a love sick teenager anymore.

"What happened back there?"

He slipped his hands into his pockets. "What do you mean?" I waited him out. "Right. I'll explain on Friday."

Back to this again. "Why can't you tell me now?"

"Because that would ruin it."

The man was making no sense. "Ruin what?"

"You'll see on Friday."

My patience was wearing thin. "What exactly are you up to?"

Calvin took my hands in his. "Trust me, okay? You'll understand everything on Friday."

"Did something go wrong at the house and you don't want me to know about it?"

"No, ma'am."

"Then what is it?"

"You'll see—"

"—on Friday," I cut in. "I don't like being kept in the dark."

He nodded. "Noted."

Maybe he'd gone ahead and done the built-ins before asking and brought them up tonight to get my reaction. Or maybe the house wasn't as far along and he didn't want to tell me how bad it would be when I moved in. But then why wait until Friday? Maybe he was trying to get as much done as possible before then.

"I've told you before I don't care how far along things are

when I move in. You've finished the bathroom, and that's all I need. You can tell me if the project is behind."

Displaying his usual patience, he kept his mouth shut.

"I'll find out on Friday." I flicked my key card against the call box and pulled the door open. "Guess I'll see you then."

Before I could stomp off inside, warm hands cradled my cheeks and he drew closer. "It'll be worth it, I promise," he whispered, close enough for me to feel his breath on my lips. Then he pressed his mouth to mine in a kiss that was slow, gentle, full of promise, and ended way too soon.

When he pulled away, I leaned forward, instinctively wanting to maintain the connection. Body reeling, I opened my eyes to find a soft expression on his face. His thumb brushed my lips before he backed away.

"See you in a few days."

Mind empty, I watched him walk back to the car and get in. I was still lingering in the open doorway as the Mercedes disappeared out of sight. Only then did I snap back to reality.

"Wow."

"You gonna close that?" came a voice from inside. "Don't you hear the alarm?"

I didn't even notice the blaring siren until she pointed it out. Quickly closing the door, I yelled, "Sorry!" Seconds later, I was inside my apartment, back pressed to the door and lips still tingling. One kiss shouldn't have short-circuited my brain like this.

I was *so screwed.*

Chapter Eighteen

Through a series of text messages with Calvin, I agreed to wait until after lunch to visit the house on Friday. After our date, I managed to clear my afternoon, which meant rescheduling two engagement sittings and one new client consult. Thankfully, all parties had been accommodating.

Not that I'd mentioned this yet. If the house was as far behind as I feared, they might plan to work over and that would take priority.

When I pulled up in front of the house, which now had amazing curb appeal, pride welled in my chest. What had been dingy, green, and neglected months ago was now shiny, white, and beautiful. Hopefully, the interior would eventually be the same.

"Hey, you," said JoJo as I approached the porch. She was sitting in a bag chair eating a sandwich by herself. "You're early. Cal said you'd be here sometime this afternoon."

He'd grossly overestimated how far my patience would stretch.

"I told him after lunch."

The young woman laughed. "It's barely twelve fifteen. After lunch is like an hour from now."

What was an hour one way or the other?

"I ate at eleven thirty." Trying to see through the big front window, I asked, "Where's your boss?"

"He'll be back." She grabbed a folded up bag chair that was leaning against the house and shook it open. "Have a seat."

I'd rather go inside, but Calvin would probably be annoyed if I went in without him. "I can do that. How are things with you?" I asked as I settled into the orange chair.

"I'm good. Ballin'. Datin' around. You know how it is."

I'd never been good at sports and couldn't remember the last time I *dated around*, but she didn't need to know that. "Right. Sure."

JoJo twisted my way. "Hey, I heard one of your friends is getting married over at Hickamore House. Is that true?"

"It is. Megan is in love with the place. In fact, I had my bridesmaid dress fitting last night. I can't believe the wedding is only two months away."

"That's so cool." She took a bite of what smelled like pastrami on rye, then set the sandwich on a napkin in her lap. Once the food was mostly down, she said, "Jas says yinz are using a tent and everything."

The name sounded familiar. "Jas?"

"Jasmine Riley. She lives here in the hood and recently started doing some admin work over at Hickamore."

The woman I met leaving his house that day. "The one who cleans Calvin's house?"

JoJo shrugged. "I don't know that she really cleans the place. It's more an excuse for him to give her money now and then."

An excuse for who? "So Calvin gives her money for nothing?"

"I don't know what their arrangement is. All I know is she's now working in the Hickamore office a couple of days a week. They got a bunch of new business and needed extra help."

That business came from Becca's company. After we'd taken the tour for Megan, Amanda moved Hickamore House to the top of her list, and even included it on her website as one of the best new event locations in town.

Calvin already told me there was nothing personal between him and Jasmine, and I believed him. But that was from his side. I had no idea how Jasmine saw the situation.

"Don't worry," JoJo said without prompting. "I don't think she's any competition for you."

"I didn't..."

She held her hands up. "I don't know what's going on with you two either. I'm just sayin'. The way Calvin's been moving lately, it's pretty clear that he's into you. So if you're interested, you don't need to worry about Jasmine. She's tried to shoot her shot, but Cal puts her off every time. The coast is clear in my opinion."

I ignored the second part and focused on the first. "The ways he's been moving?"

JoJo pointed to the house. "Like taking on this job. Our

schedule was already packed for the summer when he agreed to do this one. At first, I didn't get why we needed one more, but then I heard who owned the place and it made sense."

Calvin never mentioned other jobs. I assumed he did one at a time and had pushed to do the project because he needed the work.

"How many other jobs are you guys doing right now?"

"There are two others and a third that starts middle of next month, as far as I know. He's stretching things pretty thin. No offense, but he should have left this to someone else, because I'm going back to school in a few weeks and he'll be even more short-staffed. Good thing we're way ahead of schedule on this one."

"Ahead of—"

"Speak of the devil," she said, collecting the last of her sandwich and curling out of the chair. "Your client's been waiting for you."

Calvin tucked his keys into the pocket of his overalls as he climbed the porch steps. "I thought you were coming after lunch."

"She eats lunch early," JoJo answered for me. Turning back, she smiled. "It was nice talking to you."

"You, too," I said, but kept my eyes on Calvin. "We need to talk, as well."

As his cousin disappeared into the house, he said, "You ready to go in?"

Part of me wanted to stay right where I was and tear him a new one. Was this how he'd decided to worm his way back into my life? Or worse, maybe he saw *me* as the fixer-upper. Poor clueless Donna Bradford with the clunker car and a house that no one wanted to renovate. Must have seemed like the perfect opportunity to play the hero and come to my rescue.

But there was JoJo's last statement. They were so far ahead on the project. She'd mentioned before that Calvin had been pushing people to work overtime. His workers must have hated me. No wonder all the times I'd stopped by since Memorial Day, almost no one even looked at me let alone spoke.

No one except JoJo, and now I almost wished she'd offered the silent treatment as well.

Working hard to keep my expression neutral, I said, "I'm ready."

Brow furrowed, he asked, "Are you good? If I'd known you were coming early I'd have been here."

Of course, he would have. "I'm fine." Calvin hesitated, watching me closely, so I offered an empty smile. "Let's go in."

Like a man encountering a bear in the wild, he kept an eye on me while opening the screen door wide, then waiting for me to go in first. His movements were slow, as if he didn't want to spook me.

Too late for that.

Between being certain the project was months behind and being told they were way ahead, I had no idea what to expect when I stepped into the house. Definitely not what I saw. The place looked ready for me to move in *immediately*.

Though a two foot wide path of brown paper cut through the foyer into the living room, the floors I could see were immaculate. The exact shade of oak I wanted in the extra wide planks. The original wood work on the stairwell and railing had been re-stained and polished to a high shine.

If it weren't for the opening to the half bath that didn't exist before, I could have been stepping back in time. Moving into the living room, I couldn't believe how big it was. With the wall to the kitchen mostly gone, the open floor plan easily made the space appear double the size it truly was.

And speaking of the kitchen...

Matte finish, black stainless steel appliances contrasted perfectly with the white cabinets. The vent hood looked to be a custom piece that I'd never seen before let alone picked out. Hovering over the stove, it extended at least six inches on each side, with an oak finish that matched the floors.

The splash of wood grain in the middle of all the clean white surfaces shouldn't have worked, yet it did. Then my eyes drew down to the island and my heart stopped. The bottom was the same dark green as I'd chosen for the bathroom upstairs, and supported a thick white slab of veinless quartz. I'd only seen the small sample piece and never could have guessed how enormous and gorgeous it would be once installed.

The quartz jutted out on the left, where barstools would fit perfectly, and cascaded over the edge on the right to carry all the way to the floor. This was something out of a magazine. Throughout the process, I'd chosen countless elements from catalogues and sample books, but I couldn't have imagined this was how those choices would come together.

Remembering the timeline we'd drawn up back in May, this wasn't even supposed to be started until around the time I moved in.

Swinging around, I could only come up with one word. "How?"

What I once thought of as humility now read as smugness. "Things went well and we got more done than originally expected."

Things went well my ass. "Things going well doesn't explain being nearly a month ahead of schedule." I could only assume he'd altered the work schedule, putting the kitchen before other rooms that should have come first.

Like the studio.

Not that bringing clients into a construction zone was my best idea, but being able to take them up the new back stairs and bypass the work in progress would be my only viable option once I could no longer use my apartment.

"What got sacrificed to make this happen?"

He looked almost offended. "Nothing's been sacrificed."

"You must have changed the plan around. I needed the studio done first."

"The studio *is* done." Calvin pointed to the fireplace. "What do you think of the built-ins? They aren't permanent. I just framed that up there so you can see what it would look like."

Four foot high shelving units filled the space on each side of the fireplace beneath the two glass block windows original to the house. The wood was obviously unfinished, but other than that no one would know they weren't a permanent feature.

"They're fine," I said, still confused. "What do you mean the studio is finished?"

"We wrapped it up yesterday. I was going to save it for last, but if you want to see it now, we can head up."

"Wrapped it up?" Rubbing my hands over my face, I mumbled, "What is happening right now?"

"That's why I needed you to wait a week. So the artist could finish the job."

My hands dropped to my sides. "The artist?"

"You'll see."

Calvin spun me around and gently pushed to navigate me through the kitchen to the door in the back left corner, exactly where I'd envisioned it. On the other side was a small entryway with a another door on the right that led outside. Across from me were five hooks, I assumed for clients to hang their coats.

"Go on up."

The stairs were finished, the railing was in, and there was a sign on the door at the top that read *Donna Bradford Photography*. How...

I couldn't make my feet move. None of this was supposed to be done for weeks yet. I didn't even hear power tools being used. How could this be?

"I don't understand. You told me the house wouldn't be done until fall."

"Isn't getting done early a good thing?"

Was it? Rationally, I knew the answer was yes, but then why did everything feel so wrong?

"Come on," he said with a nudge. "You need to see the rest."

Like a robot, I climbed the stairs as ordered, head spinning.

"If you want to hang some shots on the walls here, we can put them up for you."

I'd already picked out the pictures I planned to hang in the stairwell, but I hadn't mentioned doing so, nor did I expect Calvin and his team to be part of furnishing and decorating my house.

"I'll handle it," I said, confusion and overwhelm morphing into a simmering anger.

I should have known all of this was happening. I should have been a part of it. The sign on the door was fine, but it wasn't in a font I would have picked. I'd decide whether to keep or change it once I moved in. And Calvin would not be involved.

Jaw tight, I opened the door at the top of the stairs and made the left to step over to the French Doors. The hall was larger than I'd pictured, which helped to make the space feel set off from the bedrooms down the hall.

Though at this rate, who knew what was happening down the hall, seeing as Calvin had practically gone rogue while I was too busy to stay on top of things. This was exactly what I didn't want. The house was mine. No decisions should have been made by anyone but me.

As soon as I reached for the handle on the right side door, Calvin put his hands over my eyes. "You ready?"

At my limit, I growled, "Get your hands off of me."

He obeyed immediately. "Are you mad?"

Ignoring the question, I walked into the studio. The space was huge with incredible natural light pouring in through the window I'd been dreaming about for weeks. Then I saw it. The entire right side wall was one huge mural.

In complete shock, I said, "Is that me?"

A teenage version of my face, only a hundred times larger, stared back at me. Dark curls filled what space the face didn't, and in the bottom right hand corner were the words *Black Girl Magic.*

"Yeah," Calvin said with far less enthusiasm than when we started this bizarre tour. "It's based on a picture I found in the box in the attic." He pulled a small remote from a holder on the wall next to the light switch. "There's a screen to cover it when you're doing a shoot."

A motor whirred as a screen the full width of the wall slowly lowered, covering the unexpected artwork. How much of *my* budget did that take up?

Riding a razor's edge of fury, I asked, "What's left to be done?"

He put the remote back where he found it. "The bathroom and closet off your bedroom, light fixtures, some caulking and finishing touches, and the landscaping." Looping his thumbs around the straps of his overalls, Calvin nodded toward the wall behind me. "I can have the mural painted over."

And spend more of my money to fix a decision he made? I didn't think so.

"Leave it. Will all of those things you just listed be done before I move in on the twenty-sixth?"

"That's the plan."

"Did you make any changes to what I asked for in my bathroom and closet?"

Teeth clenched, he said, "No."

Was that anger in his eyes? So the saint had a temper after all. Good for him, but I was beyond caring how he felt.

"I want a full accounting of the project so far. Is there anything else I need to see?"

Crossing his arms, he watched me with narrowed eyes for several seconds. "I thought you'd be happy."

He thought wrong. "Why did you take this job, Calvin? JoJo says you didn't need the work. She says you didn't even have time in the schedule to add another project."

"JoJo needs to mind her own business."

"Answer my question," I snapped. "Why did you push so hard for this job?"

A muscle twitched along his jaw. "I didn't push. I offered. You needed a contractor, and that's what I do. No one said you had to hire me."

That was bull and he knew it. "I didn't have a choice after all the others either turned me down or overbid. Was that your doing?"

Calvin straightened. "You think I called every contractor and told them not to take this job? Wow." He shook his head. "You think a lot of yourself, don't you?"

And we were right back where we started. "So it's a coincidence that you were my *only* option?"

"Was I, Donna? Did you talk to every single contractor, builder, and handyman in this city before hiring me? I gave you a bid just like the others, You had the choice whether or not to accept it."

Anger burned in my gut. "I had a choice, Calvin? Did I have a choice on this wall?" I asked, gesturing toward the space behind me. "Or that sign on the door, or on your crew seeing me as a spoiled bitch because you pushed them to work overtime to look like a hero? I'm not your charity case, and I never asked for special treatment. I don't need saving so keep the cape for someone else."

Without another word, he pulled out his phone, tapped the screen a few times, then put the cell back in his pocket. At that moment, my phone dinged.

"There's your accounting record. Every penny and how it was spent. I paid for the mural."

Throat tight, I stared him down. "Add it to the bill."

Dripping with sarcasm, he said, "You're the boss. If we're done here, I have work to do."

"We're done." We both knew I wasn't talking about the house.

With a curt nod, Calvin left the room. I stayed where I was as waves of anger washed over me. Anger. Hurt. And eventually a heavy ache in my chest.

I should have known better than to believe that this time would be different.

Chapter Nineteen

"What's going on?" Megan asked as she stepped into Josie's living room.

"We'll talk about it once everyone is here," our hostess said as I sat on the couch in silence.

I couldn't remember the last time I'd called for one of our meetings, but then I hadn't needed one in years. That was the blessing of being a single, self-employed woman. Not a lot of personal or emotional conundrums that required what amounted to a girlfriend 911. How had I forgotten that?

Calvin Hopkins made me forget. The jerk.

Lindsey and Becca entered seconds later as Josie grabbed a pop from the fridge for Megan. I kept my eyes on the view out the window, not yet ready to reveal how much I'd cried over the last few hours.

Thank goodness I'd cleared my schedule for the rest of the day. Photographing happily engaged couples when you'd just had your heart shredded into pieces was never fun. Or so I assumed, as I'd never tried it.

Josie grabbed two more bottles of pop for the new arrivals, and dropped a box of tissues on the coffee table in front of me.

"Oh, no," said Megan. "Is it that bad? Not Calvin."

I offered an empty laugh. "That's right. Not Calvin. Not for me, anyway."

"What happened?" Becca asked.

"I'm sorry I took you away from the baby."

She waved my words away. "He's in good hands with Jacob and Sophie, who loves any opportunity to spoil him rotten."

"Did you and Calvin have a fight?" Lindsey asked. "Is he pushing back the renovation date even later?"

If only that was the problem.

"No, he's moved it up to before I move in." My friends exchanged confused glances. "I know that sounds like a good thing, but it isn't."

Josie sat on the edge of the cushion beside me. "I'm sorry, hon, but you're going to have to explain a little more."

With a deep sigh, I went back to the beginning. "When this whole thing started, all I wanted was to find a capable contractor who could put the house back together. Someone who could create what I saw in my head while staying on budget and within my timeframe."

"And that was Calvin," Megan said.

"I didn't want to hire him, but he was the only one who didn't tell me he was too busy, or bid twice what I had to spend." Again, confusion reigned. "But he *was* too busy."

"Too busy?" Lindsey repeated. "But you just said the job is ahead of schedule."

"He had enough work for the summer. More than enough. Don't you get it?" Four sets of wide eyes stared back blankly. "He didn't need the work."

Becca tilted her head. "You only hired him because you thought he needed the work? Did he tell you that?"

"No," I had to admit. "And that's not why I hired him, but I didn't know he was making an exception for me when he took the job. In fact, he practically begged me to hire him."

"Begged you?" Josie said. "So he pretended that he needed the job and you're upset that he lied?"

Calvin hadn't technically *begged*. He'd just been persistent. I obviously wasn't explaining this right.

"The problem is that I thought one thing was happening when something totally different was happening. He didn't lie, exactly, but he didn't tell me he had multiple other jobs already booked and would have to stretch the crews thin to add mine to the schedule."

"So you're upset for the workers," Megan said. "That does sound unfair to them."

This was about more than the crew getting some overtime.

"I'm upset because I don't like being considered a charity case. I especially don't like people doing favors for me when I never asked them to, and I don't want a man who thinks he has to save me all the time. I don't need a hero. I need an equal. When Calvin made it his mission to throw this project into overdrive, without my input or permission, he crossed a line. He took over, putting me in the back seat, and I refuse to be patted on the head and taken care of like some incompetent princess."

Finally grasping the issue, they all sat back at the same time.

"That *is* annoying," Lindsey said. "He took over. How could he think that was okay?"

"I have no idea."

He *didn't* think was the only explanation I could come up with. From the start, I'd been clear about wanting to be involved in every aspect of the renovation. There were limits to what I could do. I knew that. But this wasn't a matter of who did the heavy lifting. I wasn't mad because he didn't let me help put up a wall.

I was mad because he cut me out.

"When you say ahead of schedule," Josie said, "how far ahead are we talking?"

I slouched back, hugging a baby-blue throw pillow against my chest. "It's practically done."

Megan said what the rest of them were thinking. "Isn't that a good thing?"

How did I explain this? "You love playing softball, right?"

"Yes."

"Think of it like your team is in the championship but someone told you the wrong time so when you show up the game is in the last inning. That would suck, right?"

Her face scrunched in disgust. "I'd be so mad."

"Then you get it." I made myself even sadder with the metaphor.

We sat in silence for several seconds until Becca said, "What are you going to do now?"

What could I do? "I can't exactly take the house apart again and make them do it over."

She shook her head. "You didn't bring us here because of the house. What are you going to do about Calvin?"

Suddenly exhausted, I tugged at the pillow's fringe. "There isn't anything to do about him. The house will be finished before I move in. We'll finalize the job and go our separate ways."

Megan leaned her head on Lindsey's shoulder. "That makes me sad. He had good intentions, right?"

She hadn't been so quick to forgive when Ryan deceived her. They were together now, but only because Megan was extremely forgiving and the lie turned out to be more of a misunderstanding.

Not the case here.

"His intention was to take over and make himself the hero. What I wanted didn't matter. He didn't listen. Heck, he didn't even ask. He put in a whole dang mural without even asking me. In *my* house."

"There's a mural *in* the house?" Lindsey asked.

"In the studio, yeah."

"Mural means big," Josie said. "How big are we talking?"

"An entire wall." I could still see the cartoon version of teenage Donna as big as a bus staring back at me. "And it's my face." To my horror, none of them were able to hold in their laughter. "This isn't funny."

"Your face on a wall is kind of funny," Becca said. It was ridiculous, is what it was. "Did you get a picture?"

Offended that they weren't taking this seriously, I threw the pillow aside and bolted off the couch. "No, I didn't. I'm happy I could give you all a good laugh. This is clearly a waste of time."

Before I could reach the door, Josie caught my arm. "We're sorry. Come back and we'll behave."

Reluctantly, I returned to my seat. "I don't hate the mural," I admitted. "I just hate that he did it without telling me. That's *my* studio. I should be the one who decides what goes on the walls."

Becca squeezed my knee. "I think he wanted to surprise you."

"I don't like surprises."

"He knows that now, and I doubt he'll make the mistake again."

Of that, I was certain. "He won't have the chance. I thought we were a team. I even thought he might be my person. You've all found yours, and even though I am *totally* fine being alone, for a minute there I thought I might not have to be."

Josie bumped my shoulder with her own. "If it makes you feel any better, Lindsey is alone, too."

The school teacher shot her a hard look. "By choice, and happily so." To me she said, "You liking him that much was a big deal, and it sucks that he isn't the guy you thought he was. I'm sorry, hon."

Ever the optimist, Megan said, "Maybe if you talked to him."

"We've been talking for months." I leaned back feeling completely defeated. "If he wasn't listening then, there's no chance he'd hear me now."

They patiently offered love and support as I went through my own pity party. Tears were shed, hugs given, and because they knew me better than anyone else on the planet, none of them suggested my person was still out there somewhere.

I hadn't gone looking for Calvin. If anything, I'd been subconsciously avoiding him. Avoiding romance all together, and for good reason, obviously. I really thought he was different, which made me feel like even more of a fool. Why couldn't men just be kind and supportive and sweet?

Calvin had convinced me he was all of those things, and then he turned me into a project just like the house. I didn't need to be fixed or rescued. Respect and appreciation. That's all I wanted. Was that really too much to ask?

Apparently, it was.

I WAS NOT LOOKING FORWARD to this dinner.

Since I was exactly a month out from my official move in date on the house, I'd planned to bring the renovation up during Sunday dinner. I'd also invited Calvin and let my parents know he was coming. I hadn't given a completely honest reason for bringing him along. He was the perfect person to explain to them how the neighborhood had changed, what we'd done to the house, and what the new value would be when everything was done.

A number significantly higher than what I'd paid for the place, including the renovation costs. Look at me with home equity.

Of course, there was *the other* reason. Calvin and I were dating, and I felt secure enough to break that news to Mom and Dad once they'd met the man he was today, not the kid from fifteen years ago. Except the man he was didn't turn out to be the right one after all, and finding that out *before* declaring him my boyfriend to my parents was the one plus in this situation.

Except none of this felt like a plus.

Calvin and I hadn't talked since the day of the fight. No texts. No calls. Nothing. I half expected him to send an apology message, but he clearly didn't see himself in the wrong since no such message came. Further proof that I didn't know him at all. And he definitely didn't know me.

I did send one message, but only to confirm that I was fine with the built-ins around the fireplace. He hadn't replied, but I could see that he'd read the message. Not the most mature or professional choice, but whatever. The sooner this was over and he was out of my life, the better.

"Hey there, baby," Dad said, dropping a kiss on my cheek as I walked into the kitchen. "You remembered the potato salad." Happier to see the side dish than his own daughter, he took the bowl and went straight to the silverware drawer for a fork.

"That's for dinner," Mom said.

"I'm just taking a bite." The bite was big enough that he had to strain to get it all in his mouth. Once the food was in, his big brown eyes rolled with bliss before he gave me a thumbs up.

"Is Calvin on his way?" Mom asked, handing me the plates to set the table.

"He can't make it." My voice cracked and I was grateful to be facing away from her.

Except nothing got past my mother. She followed me into

the dining room and cornered me next to the buffet. "Why can't he make it? Did you have a fight?"

Lying was pointless. "We had a disagreement on something with the house."

Technically not a lie. I attempted to avoid eye contact lest she see right through me.

Long slender fingers clasped my chin and forced me to meet her gaze. "This is more than the house. What's going on?"

Time for a diversion. "If we don't get back in there, he's going to eat all of the potato salad."

Raising her voice, Mom said, "Rodney Sinclair Bradford, you better put down that fork." The sound of silverware landing in the stainless steel sink echoed from the kitchen. "Now, tell me what happened."

There was no getting around it, so I gave a quick summary.

"When we originally started the project, Calvin said the work would take until at least October. He also led me to believe that he needed the work when he bid for the job. He didn't need the work, and he decided to push the project into overdrive to finish before I move in."

Mom blinked. "So the house will be finished early and you won't have to live in a construction zone?"

"That's right."

She stepped back and tilted her head. "This is a problem?"

"To get the house done, he pushed the crew to work overtime, giving me preferential treatment I didn't ask for, and making me look like an entitled princess after I stated multiple times that I was fine with whatever condition the house was in when I got there." Setting the dishes around the table, I added, "He also cut me out of the project entirely weeks ago without me realizing it."

"Ah," Mom said. "He took control. Typical man."

Calvin had seemed like anything *but* a typical man up to that point. "It doesn't matter. Soon I won't have to deal with him anymore."

To my great annoyance, a tear rolled down my cheek and landed on the plate I'd just set on the table. I quickly brushed it away.

"Baby," she said, turning me by the shoulders. "This is more than the house, isn't it?"

Nodding, I whispered, "I really liked him."

"Oh, darling, this is more than like. You fell for him, didn't you?" I nodded again, too choked up to speak. "Come here." She pulled me into her arms, and I started crying like a baby into her shoulder.

On Friday, I'd cried from anger. Then a wedding on Saturday had helped to keep thoughts of Calvin at bay. Mostly. But by this morning, the anger had ebbed into disappointment, and all of these feelings floated to the surface like an overwhelming tsunami of emotions.

The fragile dam I'd erected gave way the moment Mom held me close.

She patted my hair and cooed soft words against my ear until I ran out of steam and the hiccups started. That's when Dad walked into the dining room.

"What are you two doing in here? The timer is going off on the stove, and I don't know what for." When he noticed I was crying, he started backing out of the room. "I'll leave you two alone then."

Dad had never been good with tears.

"Take the roast out of the oven," Mom said to his departing back. She then wiped my cheeks with her thumb. "If he means this much to you, you need to work it out."

Not the words I expected. "Didn't you hear what I said? He took over *my* project. There's nothing to work out."

"When was the last time you felt this way about a man?"

Only one answer came to mind. "I've never felt this way before."

"Then it's worth trying. It seems to me like his heart was in the right place. Calvin likely thought that taking this task off your shoulders and going the extra mile would make you happy." With a sigh, she said, "Men don't always go about things the right way, but if you thought enough of him to open your heart, he may be worth giving an exception. At least this once."

I had to admit, there were more malicious things he could have done. "But how do I know he won't do this over and over again? I don't want to be with someone who thinks I can't run my own life."

Mom laughed. "You've always been so independent. As early as second grade, you wouldn't even let me help you with your homework. A little help isn't always a bad thing, honey. When you find the right person, you help each other."

I crossed my arms. "When has Dad ever helped you?"

"Do you think we'd be married thirty-five years if this marriage was all one-sided?"

She had a point. And I really wasn't being fair to Dad.

He'd stepped up from time to time. Nights when Mom worked late, he'd made sure I had dinner. He ordered in, but that still counted. He'd also driven me all over town to find the exact camera that I wanted, and when Bammy passed, it had been Dad's shoulder I cried on the most.

"You're more patient than I am. I want fifty-fifty."

Mom burst out laughing. "Then prepare to be alone forever Love and marriage is never fifty-fifty. It might be forty-nine fifty-one today, and ninety-ten tomorrow. But fifty-fifty is far too much to ask."

"That feels like telling me to lower my standards. Why do that when I can stay single and be happy?"

Mom crossed to the buffet, drew out the napkins, and set one beside each plate. "You can be happy alone or with someone. I'm not telling you one is better than the other, or that you can't be happy without a man." Napkins down, she looked up from across the table. "What I'm telling you is that if you care that much about this boy, then giving him a little grace might be a good idea. Just because you weren't looking for love is no reason not to fight for it when it comes your way."

The l word made the hair on my arms stand up. I said I *liked* him. I may even have had high hopes for him and considered bringing him to a family dinner, but let's not get crazy.

"You're making too much of this. I don't love Calvin Hopkins."

Mom gave a half shrug. "If that's the case, then let him go."

Since when did she give up so easily? "I *am* letting him go."

"Okay, then. Good riddance to him." She shifted a napkin half an inch to the left before saying, "We need to start eating before the roast gets cold."

Without another word, she returned to the kitchen, leaving me alone with my thoughts in the dining room. I said the words again. "I don't love Calvin Hopkins."

Feeling content with my verbal affirmation, I reminded myself that I couldn't lose something I never had. I was happily single before this mess started, and I would be happily single long after. And then I looked down to see that I'd set four places instead of three. Without thinking, I'd made a place for Calvin beside mine.

I really wanted him to be there.

Shaking the useless thought away, I shoved the napkin back in the drawer where it belonged before picking up the plate and carrying it back to the kitchen.

Chapter Twenty

"Long time no see," said JoJo as I walked up the front sidewalk to the house.

More than three weeks had passed since the day I walked through with Calvin. I'd actually been back a couple of times since then, but always well after the crew was gone for the day. Because I set up the account, I knew that the power was on, which meant I could walk around the house without feeling like a cat burglar in the dark.

I hadn't just been snooping. After seven years in my apartment, I'd accumulated more stuff than any one person needed. That meant having to decide what to keep and what to give away, and for that, I needed measurements from a few key areas to know what pieces would fit where.

The culling and packing had been a great distraction. I'd purposely kept my schedule light during August, and blocked out both the week before and the week of the move. I couldn't afford to do so for too long, as being self-employed did not come with paid time off. No pictures meant no income.

"I've been packing," I said, taking in the pretty new shrubs and the flower boxes along the front porch railing. "Whose idea was those?"

She followed my gesture to the boxes of colorful flowers. "I don't know. Didn't you order them?"

I'd spoken briefly to the landscaper, but only to say do something understated that won't require a lot of maintenance. A gardener I was not.

"Not specifically, no. Is Calvin here?"

After weeks of radio silence, I'd received a message that I could do the final walk-through today. The message didn't say whether he'd be here or if someone else would be in charge of the hand off.

"He's out back," she said. "They had an issue with the new garage door so he's got the tech here taking a look at it."

The tension that had been building since I left the house eased. "Can you do the walk-through then?"

"I don't do those." She stepped past me. "You can head out back and let Calvin know you're here though. I've gotta run. Practice starts in thirty and I was supposed to be gone twenty minutes ago."

If the house was finished, why was she even here?

"Is the house not finished?"

"It is now," she said, walking backwards. "But be careful around the trim upstairs. I just finished the touch ups."

With that she was gone. I considered going inside alone, but I also knew this walk-through had a purpose. If there was anything I didn't like, that wasn't complete, or was complete but not done correctly, this was my chance to point it out. Skipping that step meant any issues discovered later would be my problem to deal with, possibly at an added expense.

Calvin not only managed to bring the project in early, but also under budget. Despite spending an hour reviewing the itemized statement, I still couldn't figure out how he managed to do both. Still, I did not want to spend additional money later because I was too much of a coward to endure thirty minutes in the man's presence.

I made my way down the new sidewalk that led to the backyard. Thanks to the position of the house and tree coverage, this side got almost no sun, which kept it damp and grassless. Seeing as there wasn't any real parking to speak of in the back, my family and friends needed a way around that didn't involve trudging through a muddy mess.

Stepping back into the sun, I dabbed the sweat from my forehead. This August heat was going to be rough for the move, but I planned to bring over as much as I could in the next couple weeks.

Rounding the deck, which I *loved* and where I couldn't wait to have my morning coffee, I navigated the circle of chairs around the firepit, following the sound of voices coming from the garage. Peeking in, I found Calvin right where JoJo said he'd be.

"We can't have it jumping the track like this. Especially not when it's brand new. The owner is going to expect it to work like it should."

"Yes, I will," I said, joining them in the dim space.

Thanks to the shade, it was much cooler inside, which was more spacious than expected for a one car unit. My secret visits were spent inside the house so I hadn't checked out the garage. The shelving built along the back wall wasn't my idea, but as I had big plans for lots of Christmas decorations, they were going to come in handy.

Without missing a beat, Calvin said, "Donna, this is Eddie Sharp. His company installed the garage door."

"And we plan to make it work," the man said, shaking my hand. "Congratulations on your new home."

With slicked back dark hair and friendly blue eyes, Eddie was quite pretty for a man. His warm smile seemed genuine and not that of a salesman hedging for a referral, which I appreciated. My first thought was that he was exactly Lindsey's type, then I spotted the wedding ring and realized that ship had sailed.

Not that she'd have tolerated me attempting to set her up.

"Thank you," I said. "I'm looking forward to settling in."

"You've got this?" Calvin said to him.

"Yes, sir. I'll have it fixed today."

"Okay, then." He turned to me. "You ready to head inside?"

Chest tightening, I tried to relax my body, determined to hide how much seeing him affected me. "Sure, let's go."

Having Eddie as a buffer had helped to keep my nerves under control, but now the reality sunk in. I was about to be alone with Calvin in the house he made for me. With each evening visit, I noticed something new. A touch here. A detail there. All of which were his doing, not mine.

At first these finds had been annoying, but they were all things I wished I'd thought of. And now I had them. A little hard to stay mad when that was the case.

We made the trip past the firepit, up onto the deck, and

into the house without a word. In the small foyer at the base of the back stairs, cold air surrounded me, cooling the sweat along my brow.

"You want to start upstairs or downstairs?" His tone was icier than the AC.

Since I did *not* want a repeat of our last encounter, I said, "We can start down here."

He opened the door to the kitchen. "After you." By the time I reached the island, he said, "I assume you already have a list."

"A list of what?"

"Of things you want changed."

This felt very much like we'd returned to him poking the bear. "Isn't that what this walk-through is for? Why would I already have a list?"

"You've been coming by in the evenings so I assume you already know what you don't like."

There wasn't anything I didn't like. Despite his minor touches, I'd designed the whole thing, or did he forget that? But also, how the...

"Who says I've been here in the evenings?"

Calvin tilted his head to the right. "Mrs. Beaty next door. Thankfully, she called me instead of the police."

"Mrs. Beaty needs to mind her own business."

"That's never going to happen. Which is lucky for you because she's better than any security system I've ever installed."

If that was the case, I might have to invite Mrs. Beaty over for tea. Better to have her on my side than against me.

"So what if she had called the police? This is *my* house," I reminded him.

"Yes, it is. And having the police show up before you've even moved in probably isn't the first impression you want to make with your new neighbors."

Palms flat on the cool surface of the island, I struggled to keep my tone calm. This was not going to devolve into another fight. I would not give him that satisfaction.

"Are you suggesting I should have asked your permission before visiting my own house?"

Calvin shook his head, his tone matching mine. "You don't need my permission. A heads up so I could let Mrs. Beaty know would have been helpful."

If I had known that the head of the neighborhood watch group lived next door, I might have done that. Or I might have knocked on her door and introduced myself to prevent all of this. But I did *not* know about Mrs. Beaty the busybody, so I couldn't have possibly known anyone needed notification that I would be walking into *my own home*.

Seeing no point in continuing this debate, I glanced around the kitchen in silence. In fact, we could do the entire tour this way. Unless there was something I absolutely hated or couldn't possibly live with, I wasn't saying another word.

With Calvin following a comfortable distance behind, I surveyed the living room. I'd already taken window measurements, and decided I wanted the back of the built-ins painted a different color, but I would do that myself as I had yet to figure out what color.

The fireplace was beautiful, and I could already see stockings hanging from the mantel. The tree would go in front of the big picture window, which could now be seen from the outside thanks to the removal of the ugly awnings.

The truth was, I loved it. I loved every single inch of the place. The memories were still here, but the house no longer felt like the dated, crumbling structure it had become. That wasn't Bammy's counter top and her mustard colored shag carpeting was long gone, but she was still here.

Only now, so was I. Calvin had been right all those months ago. In my mind, this was Bammy's house. Looking around today, it finally felt like mine.

Breaking my silence, I turned at the entrance to the foyer and said, "Thank you."

"You don't want to see the rest?" he asked.

"I will, but I need to say something first. Thank you for doing this for me. I know you didn't have time, and I didn't always make it easy in the beginning."

"Donna—" he tried to interrupt.

"Let me get this out. It was important for me to feel like *I* did this. That's just who I am. I'm not good at asking for help, as my mother reminded me lately, but I wasn't crazy enough to believe that I could renovate the house by myself. When I saw how much you did without me, it really hurt, but that doesn't mean I don't appreciate it. So thank you. Again."

Not exactly an apology, since I still resented being left out, but none of this would have happened without him. I couldn't ignore reality.

"Are you done?" he asked, making me want to take it all back.

"You know what? Never mind." Vowing to never say

anything remotely nice to this man ever again, I stormed off toward the stairs. "Let's get this over with."

"Donna," he said, but I kept walking. "Donna," he snapped again.

"What?" I snapped back from the bottom step.

"Don't I get a turn?"

Just because he was being a jerk didn't mean I had to be one, too. Dropping to sit on the steps, I said, "By all means, go ahead." Then I braced for the argument.

"First off, you're welcome. But let's clear a few things up. JoJo wanted the summer off. Her mother said she needed to work, so I put her on this job. If she thinks she'd have had the summer off without this project, she's wrong. I'd have put her on something else. I didn't overload my schedule, or stretch my crew thin to do you a favor. I meant every word I said the last time you were here. I'm a contractor. I specialize in houses in this neighborhood. That's why I wanted the job and that's why I bid on it. Period."

"Also, the crew doesn't hate you. They're pros. They do the work and they go home, so whatever encounter you had that made you think otherwise, you misread the situation. And yes, I asked them to make sure I wasn't speaking out of turn. As for doing any of this without you, the only thing in this house that wasn't directly designed or chosen by you is the mural. I apologize for overstepping. I thought that picture was cool, and I wanted you to have a reminder of how far you've come from the ambitious teenager with your first camera to building your own business. Again, my bad for not asking first."

Like a deflated balloon, I sat on my perch unsure what to say. The only question I still had was how?

"How did you get the job done so quickly then? JoJo said you were pushing people to work overtime." I was quickly realizing JoJo was perhaps not the best source of information.

Calvin closed the distance between us and set one foot on the bottom step. "I base my timeline on worst case scenario. I'd rather tell a client six months and have it take four, than tell them four months and have it take six. If we ran into termite damage, the foundation needed reinforcing, or if we'd needed to rewire the entire house, the job would have taken longer. Whether by luck or your Bammy watching over the place, none of those things were an issue."

Reinforcing my last thought, he added, "Overtime is offered on every job when we need something done before bad weather moves in. That's nothing unusual, and the guys appreciate the extra money."

Feeling hope for the first time in weeks, I said, "So you don't see me as a charity case?"

"Did I do this job for free?"

The six-figure bill in my phone answered that one. "Definitely not."

With a sigh, Calvin rubbed a hand over his hair. "Donna, I'm well aware that you don't need me for anything. Hell, you probably could have flipped this house on your own if you'd wanted to. It would have taken about six times as long, but when you put your mind to it, you can do anything. But like with this job, I hoped you'd let me do something for you now and then. Not because you need me to, but because you want me around." Leaning forward, he braced an arm on his knee and tucked a curl behind my ear. "That's all I want. Just to be around you."

I couldn't believe it. The man even made making up easier.

Scooting to one side. I tapped the step beside me. Without hesitating, he sat down and I leaned my head on his shoulder.

"Thank you for explaining all of that."

"You're welcome. Can we make a deal that you run anything JoJo tells you past me from now on?"

"Definitely." Sitting up, I twisted so I could look into his beautiful brown eyes. "Can we also agree on no more surprises? I really don't like them."

He chuckled. "Noted."

Sitting in a comfortable silence, I turned and leaned into him again. "I'm sorry, too, by the way. I guess I have enough of a temper for both of us."

Calvin patted my leg, the heat from his palm warming my skin. "The more you trust me, the less these fights are probably going to happen. I'm willing to earn that."

I couldn't help but laugh. "How very Saint Calvin of you."

He leaned away, as if offended. "Saint Calvin?"

"You don't think that fits you?"

"I'm not thinking much like a saint with you this close."

Heat danced up my neck and warmed various other places. "Too bad there's no furniture here yet," I said, bumping his shoulder with mine. "Guess we'll have to settle for making out on these steps."

Swinging an arm over my head, he pulled me close. "You're the boss."

Trailing a finger along his stubble-covered jaw line, I held his gaze. "Thank you for making my dream come true."

He kissed my forehead. "I'll renovate a house for you any day."

With a sigh, I touched his lips. "I don't mean the house, but thanks for that, too."

Brows furrowed in confusion. "What else have I done?"

"I'll explain later. Can you just kiss me now?"

"Yes, ma'am."

My mind went blank as he did exactly what I asked. Over and over until Eddie from the garage knocked to let us know the door was working as it should. Thankfully, we were leaned back far enough on the stairs for him not to see what we were doing.

Reluctantly, Calvin left me to go deal with Eddie. Lips warm and skin tingling from his stubble, I suppressed the giggle that threatened to reveal my presence. All I could think of was those endless days of writing Donna Hopkins over and over in my notebook.

If that lovesick girl could see me now.

The girl in the mural upstairs. That daydreaming preteen was still here, only now she was a lovesick woman amazed that the boy down the street really liked her. And that he happened to be the most patient man on the planet.

Lucky, lucky me.

Chapter Twenty-One

"I still can't believe you're wearing those," Mom said, shaking her head as she unwrapped a plate and added it to the stack she'd already placed in the dishwasher.

"Why not? They're comfortable and super convenient." I whipped a marker from the front pocket of my overalls. "Need a Sharpie? I've got you. Need a box cutter?" I pulled one from my back pocket. "I've got that, too. Women have been begging for pockets for decades, and now I have seven of them. It's awesome."

The truth was, I'd been skeptical, too, until after harassing Calvin about them for the thirty-seventh time, he insisted that I try them. Going along with the joke, I pulled on a pair of his, which were ginormous on me, but dang if they weren't comfortable. And practical. I wore them to pack up half the kitchen and didn't have to go hunting for the marker not once.

I could carry everything I needed. By the time I'd packed the mugs, I had my phone, earbuds, hair tie, and even a pack of gum on me wherever I went. He totally converted me. Within a week I had multiple pairs of my own, and if I could have made them look professional enough, I'd have worn them to work.

"They're bringing in the couches," Becca said as she walked into the kitchen with baby Noah strapped to her chest in a black carrier. "You need to go tell them where they go."

A week shy of four months, the little one was turning out to be a happy baby, smiling all the time. Even with ridiculously chubby cheeks, the dimples inherited from his father were easy to see and made me want to smoosh his pudgy little face.

"You got this?" I asked Mom.

She shooed me away. "Go do whatever you need to do. I'm good."

"I'll stay and help her," Becca said, stepping around my beautiful island, which I couldn't stop sliding my hands across. It was so smooth I wanted to press my face to it.

Even after a month of going in and out for one reason or another, I still couldn't believe this was my kitchen. My house. I even had a dream in which Bammy was standing on the porch beaming with pride as she watered the flower boxes. It was like she was sending me a message that I'd done good. Before I could run to her, I woke up, which made me cry. Calvin stirred and pulled me in close.

I still didn't know if he'd been awake or reached out by instinct, but the gesture made me love him even more.

Oh, yeah. We were saying that now. Totally freaked me out when I said it first, but what was a girl to do when a man built her the most gorgeous custom desk that was exactly what she'd always wanted?

Thankfully, he'd said it back immediately, and since then we'd both said it often enough for me not to feel weird about it anymore.

"Watch this corner," Dad was saying as I walked into the living room. Calvin and Jacob were carrying my fluffy cream sofa in through the foyer, while Miles carried the coffee table.

"That goes right here facing the fireplace." I stood directly in front of where I wanted them to drop it. "Not too close to the window. The matching chairs go down there."

Found at a local secondhand shop, the chairs were the perfect size to allow for a beautiful Christmas tree to be placed right in front of the window. Though it was a muggy August day, I could still picture the house covered in holiday décor, just as Bammy had always done.

"New volunteers reporting for duty," Megan announced as she and Ryan walked into the foyer just as the guys lowered the couch. "He's the muscle and I'm the organizer. Put us to work."

Being a little over five weeks out from the wedding, the soon-to-be newlyweds had a cake tasting that morning, but had promised to join the crew as soon as they could.

"What flavor?" I asked.

"Raspberry chocolate truffle," Ryan replied. "I'll be dreaming about that cake for years."

Megan was a lemon lover so this chocolate confection must have been amazing to be the unanimous choice.

"Geraldine said to tell you hello, Calvin," she said after greeting me with a half hug. "Thank you so much for sending us her way. I don't think I've ever tasted anything that good in my whole life."

He nodded in his usual no big deal way. "Thanks for taking my suggestion."

The more time we spent together, the more I realized how generous Calvin truly was. Throughout the renovation, every company we used was owned or run by someone from the neighborhood, or they were a fledgling business in need of work and exposure.

He had a knack for knowing every mom and pop operation within a twenty mile radius, and never took the least bit of credit for the help he gave. As if he hadn't done enough for me already, Calvin also went out of his way to make me the preferred event photographer for Hickamore House.

I'd had no idea until four calls came in the same day, all for weddings at the venue. Assuming the couples had talked to Becca's office, I sent a thank you message to both her and Amanda. Neither had any idea what I was talking about.

"The chair and accent tables are next," Dad said, taking his supervisory position seriously. "Then we'll bring in the bedroom stuff."

"Where are the girls?" Megan asked while the men filed back outside.

"Becca is helping Mom in the kitchen, and Lindsey and Josie are upstairs unpacking my closet."

Closet was an understatement for what Calvin created. More like a movie star dressing room with full vanity, floor to ceiling shelves for my shoes, and enough drawers to hold everything I owned and then some. Because we'd used part of a bedroom, there was even a window. Anything on a hanger occupied the existing closet in my bedroom, which had also gotten a makeover to make it deeper than originally designed.

Megan clapped her hands. "I want to see that."

Since I'd already said where the chairs should go, and end tables were easy enough to move around if necessary, I figured the guys didn't need further directions.

"Then let's go."

Seconds later we were standing in the middle of my dream closet, which was the most organized it would ever be. The shoes were even put together by color. A red shelf, a blue shelf, a gold shelf. That had to be Josie's doing because Lindsey was the slob of our group—which she would be the first to admit—and I knew nothing in her house would ever look like this.

"She even folded your underwear," Lindsey said with disgust as they showed off their work.

"You don't fold your underwear?" Megan asked.

Josie scoffed. "She barely folds her clothes." Poking Lindsey in the arm, she said, "Tell me you pair your socks, at least."

Without shame, Lindsey rolled her eyes. "What's the point? They're all white. You just pluck two out and go."

This was the woman teaching our youth. Thank heaven she took grammar more seriously than she did the laundry.

"Your socks are paired," Josie assured me. "Should we go down and see if your mom needs help in the kitchen?"

We were only two hours into this move, but I'd been bringing boxes over for weeks so much of the work was done long before today.

"Becca is down there with her, but it couldn't hurt to have more hands on deck."

"One of us should give her a break and take the baby," Josie said as we filed out of the closet. "I volunteer for that."

"You had him this morning," Lindsey said.

"So did you."

"Not as long as you did."

Megan put an end to the bickering. "I haven't seen him yet today, so it's my turn."

This was how our visits went now. A constant battle over who got the most baby cuddles. Becca often joked that none of us wanted to see her anymore. Only Noah. Which wasn't true, of course, but the little one did have every single one of us wrapped around his tiny little finger.

Despite Becca having no biological sisters, this child had all the aunts he could ever need.

The guys were placing the end tables when we returned to the living room, and the chairs were already in place. That meant all the downstairs furniture was in. Having so much muscle was making the job move along much faster than I'd expected. The TV had been installed over the fireplace the week before, so all that was left was to fill the built-ins and hang the artwork.

Both tasks on my to-do list for the week.

"Time for a break," Mom said, carrying one side of a cooler while Becca carried the other. "The pizza should be here any minute."

The men brought the kitchen chairs into the living room since they were so sweaty, while us ladies took the furniture. I was going to need more seating as our little group of five had expanded in the last couple of years.

"So you're the lone wolf now," Mom said as she tapped Lindsey's leg. "How's it feel to be the only single one left?"

Without hesitation, she said, "I wouldn't have it any other way."

Josie laughed. "Under the word single in the dictionary, you'll find a picture of Lindsey."

"I don't blame you one bit," Mom said.

That woke Dad up. "Hey, now."

She waved his protest away and said to Megan, "How's the wedding planning coming along?"

"Wonderful, though it helps to have the best planner in town as a best friend."

"Amanda did most of the work while I was off," Becca said as she nursed Noah in a chair by the window. "But thank you for the compliment."

As everyone chatted around me, I couldn't believe I was back in this house. Bammy's soul was still here, but now I'd put my stamp on the place as well. If only she could be here to see what we'd accomplished in the home she'd loved so much.

Glancing over to the man responsible, I caught Calvin watching me with a sweet expression, and extracted myself from the couch.

"Come help me with something in the kitchen," I whispered as I strolled past him.

Heavy footfalls followed me from the room. Once we were far enough into the kitchen where no one could see us, I spun around and leapt into his arms, putting everything I was feeling into the kiss. Several seconds later, when we came up for air, he pressed his forehead to mine.

"What was that for?" His breath was warm against my cheek and I didn't even mind the sweat soaked shirt beneath my hands.

"For making this my dream home. For caring about it as much as I do." Pulling back, I looked into his eyes. "For being the perfect man for me."

"I'm far from perfect," he said with a deep chuckle that vibrated down my body.

"You're perfect *for me*," I said again, emphasizing the most important part. "That day we talked, you said that I don't need you, but I do. I need your calmness and your patience. Your creativity and practicality. You're my anchor in this crazy world, and I don't want you to ever again think that I don't need you, okay?"

Lips curling into a grin, he teased, "So you're saying you like me."

I dropped a quick kiss on his lips. "I'm saying I love you, and I hope that someday I can give you back as much as you've given me with this house."

With a deep sigh, he shook his head. "You've already given me everything I could ever want just by saying those words. For a long time, I didn't know if happy was in the cards for me. Now I do." With an affectionate squeeze, he added, "You made me work for it, but I'd do it all again because you're worth the fight, Donna. I'll always fight for you."

Knowing myself, I had to be honest. "I can't promise this is going to be easy."

"Whatever comes, we'll face it together."

Those words coming from anyone else would have triggered my inner cynic, but not from Calvin. He'd more than proven that he meant them.

"Together."

Epilogue

"I still can't believe they brought him," Lindsey growled for the third time since Becca and Jacob showed up to Megan's wedding with an extra person. And it wasn't baby Noah. I had no idea what the guy had done to her, but she acted as if they were mortal enemies.

Handing over the glass of wine I'd just procured from the bar, I followed her glare to find the technically uninvited guest dancing with a twirling ten year old on the dance floor. "What do you have against him?"

According to our brief introduction, Trey Collins was the new football coach at the high school. Becca said he was new in town, and he and Jacob had become friends. They brought him—with Megan and Ryan's approval—so he could meet new people.

I'd barely spoken to him, but he seemed nice enough.

"They put him across the hall from me," she said, staring daggers at the guy's back. "He teaches Econ and World History, and the kids love him."

None of this explained her obvious dislike.

"If a bunch of teenagers like him, then he can't be that bad."

"You obviously don't spend a lot of time with teenagers." After sipping her wine, she went on. "They only like him because he's a pushover. I'd be amazed if they learn anything in his classes."

She was right. I didn't spend a lot of time with teenagers, but I'd been one once upon a time. In my day, when we liked a teacher, it wasn't because they weren't teaching us anything. A good teacher made you want to try harder to impress them, but I wasn't going to argue the point.

"Have the kids said he's a bad teacher?"

Her lip curled in disgust. "They never say a negative word about him. He's like the reverse of a teacher's pet. He's the students' pet." Lindsey swirled her merlot. "I couldn't even get to my room the first day of school because he was holding court in the hall."

Creating a traffic jam in the hall could get annoying, but I'd seen Lindsey with her students. They adored her. She was the proctor for the drama club, and at every play I'd attended, the kids had done everything but lift her onto their shoulders and parade her across the stage.

"Don't the students like you, too?"

"Of course, they do," she said, "but not because I let them cruise by. My kids are actually learning something."

Teaching was Lindsey's passion so her dislike of Coach Collins made sense if what she said was true. I could only assume the school wanted his coaching skills enough to look the other way regarding his teaching.

At the same time, knowing that the coach and Jacob were friends made me skeptical. I couldn't picture Jacob spending time with the person Lindsey described. He was as passionate about education as Lindsey was, as well as a popular teacher in his own right.

Would he really befriend a subpar teacher? I didn't think so, but I could be wrong.

"I'm going for another piece of cake," Lindsey said, setting her glass on the table and rising to her feet. "Do you want one?"

I'd already had two slices, and Ryan was correct. The chocolate confection was the stuff of dessert dreams.

"No thanks, but the bridal party dance is coming up, so don't wander too far off."

As she strolled away, I watched Becca do a mean shimmy on the dance floor. This was her first chance to cut loose since having the baby, and it was fun to see her have such a good time. Not that she wasn't enjoying motherhood. The woman was a natural, and lucky for her, Noah had so far been a dream child.

By ten weeks he was sleeping through the night, and the only time he stopped smiling was when he needed a nap or didn't feel good. The ear infection had been rough for all of them, but once they'd cleared that up, he once again become the happy little cherub we all loved to cuddle.

"Hey, there, gorgeous." Calvin kissed my cheek before settling into the seat beside me. "You doing okay?"

"I'm good. How about you?"

When the day started, Calvin had been surprisingly nervous. The schedule of Hickamore House bookings had filled up nicely in the last few months, but this was the first event of this magnitude to actually take place. The rest were either later in the year or as far off as next summer.

"One issue with a soda canister, and we'll need to work on overflow parking," he said, "but the rest is good so far. Has Megan said anything?"

Mr. Calm had been replaced with a stressed out man I hardly recognized. "Honey, relax. The ceremony was beautiful, and everyone is having a great time. You're a guest tonight. Sit back and enjoy yourself."

"They have no complaints?" he asked, not the least bit appeased by my words.

Cupping his cheeks, I held his gaze. "Calvin Hopkins, you've created a stunning event venue, paid attention to every single detail, and made it possible for one of my best friends to have the wedding of her dreams. Take a breath. Hickamore House is perfect."

"You're sure?"

Oh, how I loved this man. "I'm positive."

"Let's go," said Josie, as she took us each by the hand. "You can kissy face later. Right now it's all bridal party to the floor."

"I'm not in the bridal party," Calvin reminded her. I'd worried Calvin would feel left out, but I should have known the girls would never let that happen.

Blonde curls danced around her face as she shook her head. "You're an honorary member. Ryan's cousin had to leave early, so Donna needs a partner and you're it."

The moment we stepped foot on the dance floor, the DJ rolled into an old school Mary J. Blige song and Calvin pulled me close against him. With his cheek pressed to my temple, we swayed with the music, our bodies moving in time as if we'd been dancing together for decades. Where he led, I followed, and that's how our life together would always be.

Leaning back, I smiled up at him. "You're good at this."

"I've got some moves." He spun, leaned me deep over his arm, then twirled me upright again. "See that? You didn't know I had that in me, did you?"

"I did not." Laughing, I flattened my hand over his heart. "Is there anything you *can't* do?"

With a quick nod, he said, "Let you go. That's the one thing I can't do."

Heart melting, I patted his black lapel. "I'm not going anywhere."

Amazed I could feel so blissfully happy, I set my chin on Calvin's shoulder and spotted Coach Collins dancing with Lindsey. From the way he held her, I suspected that the coach felt very differently about Lindsey than she felt about him.

"Interesting," I said aloud.

"What's that?" Calvin asked.

"Lindsey is dancing with Trey Collins."

My partner spun us around so he could see what I saw. "He's been watching her all evening."

"He has?" I needed to pay more attention.

"Yeah, I noticed it a couple hours ago."

Curious about his opinion, I said, "Have you talked to him?"

"A bit. Seems like a nice guy."

"No bad vibes or inappropriate comments?"

Calvin spun us again. "Not around me. He said some nice stuff about the house, and then we talked football until I got called away to handle the canister issue."

Lindsey hated sports. "They're total opposites so I don't see anything happening between them."

"We're kind of opposites, aren't we?"

I didn't think so. "You and I are different, but not opposites. Lindsey would rather set herself on fire than talk about football. And anyway, she really doesn't like him."

With a chuckle, he said, "You didn't like me very much six months ago."

True, but that was based on teenage idiocy.

"I only felt that way because I thought you didn't like me, remember?"

"And you were very wrong." He pressed his cheek to mine and whispered, "I like you very much, and I always have."

Leaning into him, I closed my eyes. "I like you very much, too. And I always will."

———

THANK you so much for reading Not So Easy. I hope you enjoyed Donna and Calvin's story as much as I enjoyed writing it. If you don't want to miss the last book in the series coming later this summer, head over to Amazon and pre-order Love Me Not now!

Other Books By
Terri Osburn

Anchor Island Series

Meant To Be

Up To The Challenge

Home To Stay

More To Give

Love On Anchor Island

In Over Her Head

Christmas On Anchor Island

An Anchor Island Collection (Books 4, 5, & 6)

Ardent Springs Series

His First and Last

Our Now and Forever

My One and Only

Her Hopes and Dreams

The Last In Love

Shooting Stars Series

Rising Star

Falling Star

Wishing On a Star

Among the Stars

The NOT Series

Not You Again

Not Playing Fair

Not Going There

Almost Not a Wedding

Not So Easy

Love Me Not (coming Fall 2024)

Stand Alones

Ask Me To Stay

Wrecked

Awakening Anna

Love Me, Cowboy

About the Author

Amazon #1, Wall Street Journal, and USA Today bestselling author Terri Osburn writes contemporary romance with heart, hope, and lots of humor. Her work has been translated into five languages, and has sold more than 1.5 million copies worldwide. She resides in Pittsburgh, PA with two frisky felines, and two high-maintenance terrier mixes. Learn more about this international bestseller and her books at www.terriosburn.com.